Powerful

ALSO BY LAUREN ROBERTS

Powerless

Powerful

LAUREN ROBERTS

SIMON & SCHUSTER

First published in Great Britain in 2024 by Simon & Schuster UK Ltd

7 9 10 8 6

Simon & Schuster UK Ltd
1st Floor, 222 Gray's Inn Road
London WC1X 8HB

Simon & Schuster: Celebrating 100 Years of Publishing in 2024

www.simonandschuster.co.uk
www.simonandschuster.com.au
www.simonandschuster.co.in

Simon & Schuster Australia, Sydney
Simon & Schuster India, New Delhi

A CIP catalogue record for this book is available from the British Library.

PB ISBN 978-1-3985-3573-2
eBook ISBN 978-1-3985-3575-6
eAudio ISBN 978-1-3985-3574-9

Printed and Bound in the UK using
100% Renewable Electricity at CPI Group (UK) Ltd

MIX
Paper | Supporting
responsible forestry
FSC® C171272
FSC
www.fsc.org

To the girls with softer dreams — your purpose is just as powerful!

RECORDED ELITES

MUNDANES

DEFENSIVE

OFFENSIVE

KNOWN RECORDED ELITES

*'Wielder - sense and use others'
abilities within proximity - 1*

ABILITIES › 100

MUNDANES
Amplifier - voice projection › 100
Bluff - lie detection › 200
Hyper - enhanced senses › 250
Scholar - intellectual › 100
Sight - video recording & projection via eyesight › 100

DEFENSIVE
Blink - teleportation anywhere in sight › 100
Crawler - wall scaling › 225
Healer - quick healing › 100
Illusionist - illusion creation › 100
Shield - purple force field creation › 170
Shimmer - light manipulation › 125
Transfer - infuse objects with abilities › 100
Veil - invisibility › 130

OFFENSIVE
Blazer - flame manipulation › 200
Bloom - plant manipulation › 130
Brawny - physical strength › 250
Cloner - clone creation › 110
Dual - two-ability wielding › 100
Gust - air manipulation › 125
Hydro - water manipulation › 150
Ignite - explosion creation › 100
Shell - skin of stone › 125
Tele - object movement via mind › 100
Volt - electricity manipulation › 100

FATALS - 1 OF EACH IN POSSESSION OF THE KING
Controller - manipulate others - 1
Mind Reader - 1
Silencer - smother abilities of others - 1

PROLOGUE

Adena

FIVE YEARS AGO

The biggest man I've ever seen is barreling behind me.

Then again, it is likely that I'm exaggerating. Mama always did tell me what a curse it is to be blessed with such an overactive imagination.

I would hate to proclaim that he's the largest man I've ever seen if he isn't truly worthy of the title. So, I dare a glance over my shoulder, dodging carts and jutting cobblestone beneath the boots swallowing my feet. Mama said I would grow into them. I'm still waiting for that day.

No, that is definitely a giant man. The white mask

he wears leaves the bottom half of his face exposed, displaying red cheeks and a twisted scowl between each panted breath.

A tangled strand of hair whips me in the face when I turn back towards the street sprawled before me. Several curls crawl into my mouth when a rare gust of wind decides to rush down Loot Alley on its way to somewhere far more important. I lift a hand to swipe at the unruly strands, only to be reminded of the very reason I'm running from an Imperial in the first place.

Honey oozes between my fingers, dripping lazily from the sticky bun squished in my palm. I might have gotten away with my first attempt at thievery if it weren't for the fact that I'd tripped into the very stand I'd tried to steal from.

Unfortunately, it only got worse from there.

I then profusely apologized for stealing before spinning on my heel and running off. This got the merchant's attention, then the Imperial's, and now everyone on the market street is bearing witness to the scene I'm causing.

It's not as though the Imperial – or the king he serves – cares about the overcooked dough I sloppily stole. No, it's the example that he is chasing. The spectacle I will become at the bloody post in the center of Loot. Imperials like their whips, and I like my sticky buns. And, for some reason, the starving girl is in the wrong.

Men, women and wandering children jump out of my path, though most look unfazed by the sight of me hurtling past. Looting on Loot is hardly uncommon. Merchants curse as I weave between their carts, though I shout my apologies at anyone who cares to accept them.

This may be the most terrifying thing I've ever done.

I mean, attempting to sew a pleated skirt was certainly a daunting task. But the threat that pointy needles pose likely pale in comparison to what this Imperial has in store for me.

I glance down at the sticky bun that is, in fact, feeling like its name suggests.

What has gotten into me?

I shout an apology to the woman scurrying out of the way, likely swallowed up by the sound of her cursing my name.

Hunger. That's what has gotten into me.

But I don't particularly like being cursed at. In fact, if most of the people yelling in my direction actually got to know me, I'm sure I would make a completely respectable impression under different circumstances.

Hair flinging over a shoulder, I peek at my giant pursuer. Face still red as ever, he charges persistently.

Well, he's definitely not a Flash, that's for certain.

When my head swivels back towards the street, it's glinting silver that catches my eye.

The girl stands in my path, staring curiously at the scene sprinting towards her. Silver hair spills from her head, pouring down her back. And if I make it out of this unscathed, I'm determined to find a fabric of the same shimmering shade.

I admire her hair until it is suddenly right in front of me. She hasn't moved, and I'm not planning on slowing down. So, without a second thought, I run right into her.

Well, technically, I run right *through* her.

Despite my many years of being able to pass through matter at will, the tingling sensation never fails to send a shiver down my spine. I have yet to get accustomed to the ability I possess – a result of the Plague that swept through Ilya and formed the generations after into Elites.

I don't dare look back until I hear a heavy thud hit the

cobblestones behind me. I barely catch the Imperial's face hitting the stones before the girl is bounding behind me.

'Don't stop!' she shouts, not bothering to fight the smile pulling at her lips. All I can manage is a breathless laugh in response as I focus on forcing my tired legs faster.

We run until she yanks me down a narrow alley, dodging the huddled homeless. 'This way,' she orders, continuing to tug on my arm. It's only after slinking down several shadowed alleyways that we allow ourselves to lean against a grimy brick wall, gulping down equally dusty air.

She looks over at me, and I look over at her.

Something like understanding seems to settle between us. As though loneliness has found its equal.

The girl raises her eyebrows at the sticky bun still gripped in my hand. 'First time stealing?'

'That obvious?' I smile sheepishly.

She shrugs. 'You would think a Phaser would be better at escaping.'

'See,' I say with a sigh, 'that's what I thought. And look at where it got me.' There is a stretch of silence before I blurt, 'Oh, and I'm not really sure what you did back there, but thanks for your help.'

She flashes a smile. 'Nothing difficult. Just stuck my foot out. It's the Imperial's fault for running into it, really.'

We laugh. It's nice, this brief moment of companionship. The warmth coats my chest when I giggle for the first time in a long while. For the first time since Mama.

I raise the sticky bun between us. 'Wanna split?' She laughs again when I wave the dough beneath her nose.

'What, with your sweat all over it?'

'Oh, this is nothing,' I say, the words muffled by the bite I take. 'I've sweat more while trying to stitch up a corset.'

She looks absolutely distraught at that statement. 'Why would you ever need a corset?'

'Unfortunately,' I sigh wistfully, 'I wouldn't. But richer people do.'

She blinks at me, something brewing behind her blue eyes. 'You sell clothes?'

My eyes skim down the dirtied shirt hanging from her shoulder to land on the pants bunched at her boots. 'Yeah, and it looks like you could certainly use some.' I run a hand down her sleeve, feeling the coarse fabric rubbing against her skin. 'No, this won't do at all.'

'Stealing food is kind of my priority at the moment,' she grumbles.

Excitement bubbles up my throat in the form of a hushed shout. 'You steal? Like, steal good?'

'Steal good?' she echoes skeptically.

'Well, whatever I just did was bad.' She is quick to nod in agreement. 'So, can you do what I did, but, like, good?'

'Anything is better than that,' she says with an amused smile. 'But yes, I steal *good*.'

'Perfect,' I say cheerily before sticking out the hand currently unoccupied with my stolen goods. 'I'm Adena.'

She takes my hand, seemingly shaking it just to humor me. 'I'm Paedyn.'

'Well, Paedyn—' I rip the sticky bun in half, offering a smushed side to her — 'I think we could make a great team.'

She pops a piece of dough into her mouth. 'So, you sew, and I steal? We share the money and the food?'

'Exactly.' I hesitate for a moment. 'I mean, unless you have somewhere better to go than the slums . . .'

'Not anymore,' she says a bit too quickly. 'So,

partners?'

'Partners.' I smile before looking down the length of her. 'And my first order of business is getting you into something far less horrendous.'

She huffs out a laugh. 'Yeah, because that's a priority.'

I take another bite of sticky bun, humming at the sweet honey melting on my tongue. 'And your first order of business,' I mumble between bites, 'is getting me more of these.'

CHAPTER 1

Makoto

Her name is on a list of the dead.

I squint into the stinging sunlight, scrutinizing every name inked onto the banner. Hers sits among the eight others, likely overlooked beneath the prince's crowning the top. But despite being on the list, our future Enforcer will easily evade the death awaiting the other contestants. Because these Trials were made for Elites like him. Not Elites like her.

My eyes skim over the list once again, recognizing no other names. I've never been one to keep up with which Elites manage to wrangle enough relevance to make it into the Trials.

A shoulder collides with mine, followed by several other limbs pushing against me. Loot is swimming with sticky bodies and echoing shouts of celebration, further adding to the list of reasons why I would rather be anywhere else but the slums of Ilya. It's a struggle to push my way through the crowded street, every inch of it crawling with ignorance incarnate. Every inch cheering for each contestant they chose to represent Loot.

I push through the crowd, ignoring their celebrations.

They have done nothing more than send Mundanes and Defensive Elites to their deaths.

And she is one of them.

But it should be me. Me who dies brutally. Dies alone. Dies at all.

Chants in honor of the sixth ever Purging Trials ring in my ears, each word a reminder of what I've done – nothing.

I've spent my whole life huddling in her shadow, hiding from life itself. And now she has been chosen simply because she did nothing of the sort. The people knew her, loved the street magic she performed as a Veil. And yet, they sentence her to death under the guise of honor.

She is a Defensive. Therefore, she is dead.

And I need to find her.

My hands are streaked with coal dust, leathers clinging to my sweaty body as though I'm still hammering steel over a scalding fire. I had worked through the night and was continuing still when the commotion managed to drag me from the shop.

I should have gone to see her last night. Should have been there when she found out.

And now I'm shoving through a sea of people, attempting to find her before it's too late. I scan the packed street, catching sight of a coach rumbling towards the end of it. It screeches to a halt, the horses nearly as impatient as the drivers, eager to escape the slums.

I sure as hell know how that feels.

I'm shoved forward when the congested crowd begins flocking towards the coach, clustering it as though they're offering free rides out of this shithole. Begrudgingly, I allow myself to be swept forward, managing to catch a glimpse of her climbing inside.

An Imperial ushers her up the step, and in typical Hera fashion, she shyly thanks him as though he's not escorting her to her doom. Her sleek black hair is the last thing I see before she's swallowed by the four walls, sitting in the belly of the coach.

The world seems to quiet, slow its spinning with each shaky breath I manage.

I didn't get to say goodbye.

My thumb finds the scar cutting crookedly through my lips, tracing it like I had the day my life truly became a secret. A familiar numbness begins to bleed over my body, bathing every bit of me in bitterness.

I'm about to turn away, unable to watch her be paraded towards her death.

That's when a flash of silver catches my eye.

I peer over the dozens of heads dotting the street, watch her walk towards the coach with hair that tells me all I need to know.

So, this is the famous Silver Savior.

Word of her saving Prince Kai managed to reach even my ears – evidence of how significant she's become amongst the slums. Perhaps I'm a skeptic, or simply the only logical person living in the vicinity, but I'm not entirely convinced by her battle with a Silencer. A battle that the future Enforcer himself couldn't win.

And I know exactly what it's like to be in Kai's shoes.

I'm watching her climb into the coach when a hopping figure captures my attention. Dark curls bounce with each attempt to see over the crowd. Her hands are raised, waving haphazardly at the Silver Savior. She's shouting something that looks quite heartfelt, likely a wasted goodbye that will never be heard.

I lean over a pair of young women who are chanting terribly off-key to the rest of the street. Squinting, I struggle to scan the girl's face with how persistently she's bouncing. Her features grow more blurry with each hop off the ground, making it difficult to focus on them. But something about her seems faintly familiar, as though this isn't the first time I've been graced by the presence of her perpetual perkiness.

I roll my eyes when recognition rams into me.

Oh, I know exactly who this is. In fact, I believe she even made it onto my ever-growing list of reasons to never leave my shop.

I was buying supplies from a merchant who was just as eager to take my money as I was to retreat back into my glorified shed. It was with a bundle of leather tucked beneath my arm and a severe lack of pep in my step that I heard the most absurdly bubbly sales pitch.

And that's when I saw her, curly hair bouncing with each energetic bob of her head. A plethora of clothing piled around her while she described what is commonly known as a blue shirt with about a dozen more words than necessary.

I may have said a thing or two, though the details of our conversation were hardly interesting enough for me to waste time recalling now.

That was several weeks ago now, but there is no mistaking that the girl currently waving a crazed set of hands down the street is the same seamstress who sells on the corner of an alley.

And she's a Phaser. I know that much about her. Well, that, and her astounding ability to never tire of talking.

I watch her blow kisses to the Silver Savior, so many that I brace myself to witness her faint. But she does nothing of the sort, leaving me to continue watching the endearing embodiment of her affections for this girl.

There is no mistaking the sincerity in each flailing wave and shouted sentiment. This seamstress knows the Silver Savior, and quite personally by the looks of it. Likely enough to do just about anything for her.

My mind races recklessly, scheming. A horribly impulsive plan begins to form, one that should likely never leave the confines of my mind, let alone be executed at all.

But this just might work.

That is typically what one thinks right before everything goes to shit.

Then again, one might argue that things couldn't possibly get any shittier.

CHAPTER 2

Adena

Scraps of fabric are my only company.

The whole thing sounds far more depressing than it is, really. This is a very temporary state of loneliness. Once Pae returns from the Trials – because I refuse to believe there is any other outcome – she will be back to sleeping soundlessly on my left.

I scoot over at the thought, ensuring there is plenty enough space for the presence of her to sleep peacefully. I refuse to occupy her side and, instead, reserve it with my pile of fabric. A memorial, if you will. But not in a dead, depressing way. More like an 'I miss you and, don't worry, I'm saving your spot' sort of way.

The Fort is a bit drafty tonight, though that's likely due to the fact that we constructed it from dozens of miscellaneous items at the age of thirteen. The sudden urge to give our little home a makeover has me far too giddy to sleep. Pae deserves a more fabulous Fort to come home to. Though I suppose she'll be able to buy half the slums if she happens to win these Trials.

How remarkable would it be if she manages it? Manages to win what is meant to showcase the Elite power, yet she has nothing of the sort. But if any Ordinary could, it would be Pae. She will fool them all with her 'Psychic' abilities, because if she hadn't told me otherwise, I likely would still believe her act of observance.

I burrow into our blanket, my mind buzzing with possibilities. And then I nod to myself, settling on my Fort redecoration surprise. This will be my gift to her.

I hadn't realized I'd drifted asleep until a ray of sun tickles my forehead.

Rolling over, my face finds the mound of scraps to be rather comfortable before the strands have me sneezing. Once my nose has finished throwing its fit, I sit up, brushing back the bangs sticking to my forehead. My sleepy eyes are slow to open but quick to find the spot beside me empty.

I stutter from where I sit behind the Fort, unsure of what to do with myself. For the past five years, Paedyn has only woken up due to my perseverance each morning. And, maybe a part of me reveled in the routine of it, of being the first person she sees. Though, the task is certainly not for the faint of heart. She's stubborn, even in sleep.

With resolve I'd rather not muster at the moment, I manage to get to my feet. Exchanging one oversized shirt for another, I attempt to run fingers through the tangled curls earned from a night of tossing and turning. It's not long before I give up, as I do each day. I've decided it is now part of my routine.

After twisting my hair into a messy knot at the nape of my neck, I gather a bundle of clothes into my arms and phase right through the barrier that is our Fort.

Sunlight coats the tops of crumbling shops as I set out onto Loot, its rays creeping down the walls to splatter the pavement. I smile at the sight before silently saying good morning to the shiny star. We've always been close, connected in a way I can't explain.

I pass several merchants preparing their carts for the day, smiling at the few who appreciate the gesture.

Routine. Again.

I've nearly made it to my corner when the smell of fresh dough wafts towards me. My stomach complains loudly at the scent, grumbling about its lack of food. And apparently, my feet listen. They carry me towards the source of the smell while I hug the mass of fabric tighter against me.

That's how I find myself standing before a merchant's cart, piled high with sticky buns. The man nods curtly while I smile sweetly as though I'm not considering anything unlawful. But it's as though the temptation was created just for me. My stomach is insistent, my hands greedy to snatch a glazed piece of dough.

I never have been much good at snatching, hence why I've always left that area of expertise to Pae. But she's left me alone with my appetite and no voice of reason. What a dangerous combination. And my hunger is currently drowning out all rationality.

So, when the merchant's back is turned, I repeat history.

I steal a sticky bun.

The honey seeping between my fingers feels like the embodiment of déjà vu. I stare at it glistening in my palm while struggling to clutch my bundle of clothing beneath a single arm. Turning away slowly, I whisper an apology to the seemingly kind man as I step away from his stand.

That is when the green pleated skirt I spent hours stitching falls from the pile, landing behind me. I spin on my heel, bending to pick it up before the merchant notices and—

'Hey! You got money for that, girl?'

I stumble into a run.

I'm a terrible person who steals and runs from the consequences. Not that Pae is a terrible person. No, I'm just not cut out for this. My conscience can't condone this sort of dreadful deed.

'I'm sorry!' I shout as I tear off down the street. 'I'm sure it's delicious and very much worth the money I don't have!'

I weave through the growing crowd, feeling the clothes slipping with each bounding step. Blurry faces watch me race by, one of them partially covered with a white mask.

Perfect. I've caught the attention of an Imperial.

Just as I had five years ago for the exact same crime.

I could laugh at my repeated stupidity. Except, Paedyn isn't here to save me this time around, leaving me no other option but to run alone and attempt to escape my crime.

The Imperial is now in pursuit behind me, shouting orders to stop my sprinting. Forcing myself to ignore his threats, I run by the familiar alley that has our Fort tucked inside. It physically pains me to throw my clothes towards the dead end, but I offer them a reassuring, 'I'll come back for you!' And then I'm squeezing my eyes shut so I don't have to witness the sight of my beloved clothing plummeting towards the dirty cobblestone.

Free from the bundle, I race down the street while mentally scolding myself for what I've done. Though, that doesn't stop me from scarfing down several bites of dough as I try to lessen the amount of incriminating evidence.

I turn down several streets, cutting through alleys while attempting not to choke on my stolen goods. The Imperial is still on my heels when I skid round a corner and—

Large arms wrap round my body, pulling me against a foreign one. My attempt to struggle is futile in comparison to the size of this someone behind me. I'm about to yell for anyone who might care enough to help when a hand suddenly clamps over my mouth, smelling of a sort of soot that stings my nose.

I'm being pulled backwards, farther and farther

until my captor collides with the wall and—

And phases right through it, forcing me to do the same.

I stumble on the other side of the brick, my feet fumbling beneath me. A muscled arm is lifting me off the floor before I can slip and fall face-first into it. A large hand still covers my nose and mouth and I'm desperately trying to free myself so I can spew every word that's being smothered.

That's when I sneeze into the palm.

'Shit!'

My feet have only just returned to the floor before I'm being shoved away from the source of that deep voice, my nose still burning from the dust covering his hand. I take a deep breath before turning to face him, attempting to collect my thoughts and rein in my emotions.

But it seems I do neither of those things, because I spin on my heel at the same moment I harshly whisper, 'You're a Phaser, too?'

If I had a single rational thought left, it vanishes when I lay eyes on him.

If there is a God, this man is certainly proof that He has His favorites.

He's breathtaking in the way I would imagine a stab wound to be, so handsome it's piercing. Like a blade, everything about him is sharp and cold.

And suddenly I have a vague sense of familiarity at the sight of him.

Tipping my head up, my eyes find his dark ones before trailing down to the sharp cheekbones beneath them. I follow the curve of his Cupid's bow until my gaze traces the scar slicing through his lips. Everything below his face is hidden beneath thick, partially leathered clothing, though the sheer size of him is obvious. His dark sleeves are sloppily rolled to his elbow, displaying muscled arms streaked in the black dust that made me—

'You sneezed in my hand.' His arm is stretched out in front of him as he blinks down at his palm in disbelief.

'Well . . .' My whole body flushes as I struggle to form words. 'Your hand made me sneeze.'

'You don't say? I hadn't noticed.' He says this with a stony sort of sarcasm while running his palm down the side of his pants.

I stiffen slightly at his tone, but at the reminder of my poor first impression, I force myself to smile in the hopes he will offer one back. 'Sooo,' I say slowly, drawing out the word, 'you're a Phaser?'

With the hand unmarred by my sneeze, he combs long fingers through dark hair. It's parted and shaggy and likely long enough to partially tie back with a strap. But when he brushes the strands out of his face, I catch sight of a silver streak hiding amongst the rugged black waves.

My heart stops at the sight. At the reminder of Pae.

'Was walking through the wall not proof enough of that?' he asks blandly, his eyes finally flicking to mine.

I doubt I'll be getting so much as a smile any time soon. Or a kind word for that matter. But that doesn't mean I can't try to earn one.

'Sorry, um, I've just never met another Phaser before.' I smile despite the stony expression he wears. 'I mean, obviously I knew there were others. I'm not special enough to be the only one. Although—'

'See, as incredibly interesting as wherever the hell you were going with that is, we need to get down to business.' He pairs a solemn nod with what he likely thinks is a sympathetic look. 'So, I'm gonna go ahead and let you ask one more question before I dive into everything.'

I blink at him, temporarily dazed. 'Excuse me?'

He raises his eyebrows. 'Are you sure that's the question you want to ask?'

'W-What business are you talking about?' I sputter. 'What is going on?'

'All right, that's two questions. So, pick which one you like more.'

We stare at each other.

I can only imagine what Paedyn might have done at this point, and it most definitely involves a dagger. But I choose a far less violent approach – maybe I can annoy him out of my life.

I take a deep breath before plastering a smile onto my face. 'Fine,' I say sweetly. 'Could you stick your hand through the wall for me? I've just always wanted to see someone else do it.'

He lifts a hand to run it down his face. 'Honestly, I shouldn't even be surprised.'

I wait until he's walked towards the brick and stuck out a hand. 'Oh, wait.' I giggle innocently while he takes his time turning towards me. 'Not that wall. No, I wanted you to stick your hand through that one.'

I point towards the bricks opposite him, earning a sarcastic grin from the nameless man I'm not sure I wish to see again. When he reaches my wall of choice, he turns to raise an eyebrow. 'Do you have a hand preference? Perhaps the one you sneezed on?'

'No, that would be silly!' I laugh lightly.

His left hand reaches for the wall.

'On second thought, your right one.'

He turns stiffly, barely containing his abundance of annoyance. 'Any other requests? Maybe stick my head through as well? A foot?'

I shake my head, smiling a bit too widely. 'Nope!'

He turns back towards the wall. Several heartbeats pound past in which he simply waits. After throwing a glance over his shoulder, he deems it safe to finally slide his hand through the wall. I watch it disappear onto the other side, smiling at the familiarity of it all. It's oddly comforting, finding someone with the same power running through their veins. No matter how rude they seem to be.

After freeing his hand from the wall, he throws me a tired look. 'Satisfied?'

I cross my arms over my chest in an attempt to seem intimidating. 'And if I'm not?'

'Life is abundant with disappointment, I'm afraid.' He strides back over to me, voice deep and tone dull. 'Now, it's time I tell you why I saved your ass.'

I pin him with a questioning look. 'Yes, I have been wondering that. Because I'm getting the impression that it certainly wasn't out of the goodness of your heart.'

'Obviously not.' He crosses stained arms over his leathered chest. 'Speaking of, why the hell didn't you just phase into a building and lose the Imperial?'

With a sudden urge to defend myself, I lift my chin. 'Well, I . . . I never know what's waiting on the other side.'

I am then distracted by my dim surroundings, as though seeing them for the first time. We are standing in a crumbling building, deserted by everything but whatever creatures are likely crawling around.

He stares at me for a stressful few seconds before stating, 'Odd.'

I can feel his eyes lingering over the length of me and would rather not know what it is he's seeing. Possibly the sweat dotting my brow, or better yet, the mop of tangled hair falling from its already messy bun. I run my sticky hand down the side of my pants self-consciously, trying to rid it of the remaining honey clinging to my palm.

When he finally looks away, his tone is suddenly serious. 'All right, I . . . I need your help.'

He all but rolls his eyes at the sight of my spreading smile. 'Sorry, could you say that one more time?' I ask sweetly with a hand cupped around my ear.

There's that mock sympathy seeping onto his features once again. 'Not a chance. You're all out of questions, hun.' Taking a deep breath, he begins pacing absentmindedly. 'You're a seamstress, yes?'

'How do you know I'm—' My words stop the moment my heart seems to do the same. I blink at him, his features suddenly shifting into something undeniably familiar. My gasp has him startling in surprise, pressing a hand over his heart. 'You! I know you!'

His eyes dart away from mine, guilty in the way they pointedly avoid my gaze. 'I thought you looked familiar,' I blurt before poking an accusing finger into his chest. 'You're the one who shouted at me on the street!'

He shrugs nervously, scratching a hand against the back of his shaggy hair. 'I would prefer to call it constructive criticism, but I can see how—'

'Well, you *criticized* my favorite blouse.'

'And I stand by what I said. It should have been—'

'Red,' I finish through my teeth. 'Yeah, I remember.'

He looks as though he might actually laugh. 'Well, have you sold it yet?'

I'm unable to look at him as I grumble, 'No, the customer agreed with you.'

He shuts his eyes, fighting some internal battle that has him blowing out a breath. 'How incredibly unfortunate for you that they had good taste.'

My teeth grind together, the feeling foreign and full of frustration. This man is, so far, slightly insufferable. I've never met someone so completely cold and condescending. It's impressive, really, his ability to ruffle even me.

The thought suddenly has me setting my jaw along with a new goal for myself. I hereby refuse to give him the satisfaction of irritating me.

And that is why I scare him with a wide smile as I say, 'So, why is it you need my help?'

It takes him a moment to recover from my sudden shift of emotion. 'Look.' He sighs. 'Someone very important to me just got sent into the Trials.' His eyes search mine. 'You know exactly what that's like.'

'How do you . . . ?' I trail off, confusion crinkling my brow. 'How do you know that?'

'I was out on the street when the coach pulled up to take the contestants to the castle.' He clears his throat. 'I watched Hera climb in before the Silver Savior followed. And that is when I saw you, jumping and waving at her like she was your everything.'

'That's because she is,' I whisper.

'Well, I don't know about you, but I never got to say goodbye to my everything.' He spits out the words as though they left a bitter taste in his mouth. 'Hera won't make it through these Trials. And that is why I need your help.'

I pair a sympathetic look with a shake of my head. 'What could I possibly do?'

He steps towards me, swallowing the distance between us. 'I need to get into the castle and see her one last time. There's something I need to give her.' The words tumble from his mouth, urgent and more earnest than any one prior. 'I know it might sound crazy, but if you can make me look like an Imperial, I can phase through the walls and walk around the castle without fear of getting caught.'

My lips part as shock smothers every other emotion. 'You want me to disguise you as an Imperial?'

'Do you have a better idea?' he counters.

I quickly come to the conclusion that I do not, in fact, have a better idea. Each of my hands finds a hip as I look up at him stubbornly. 'And why would I want to help you? You haven't exactly made a good first impression.' I pause. 'Either of the times we've met.'

'Well, my charm isn't for everyone.' He sighs, lifting a hand to run his thumb over the scar splitting his lips. 'But I assure you, this would be mutually beneficial.'

I frown. 'How so?'

'For starters, it's very clear that you need . . . help.' I'm about to object when he raises a sooty hand, stilling my tongue. 'Need I remind you of your little attempt at thievery just now?' He tsks, giving me a disapproving shake of his head. 'I can offer you food. Water. Supplies. All of it.'

How incredibly tempting. Plague knows I won't last long without Paedyn here to steal me sustenance. I shift on my feet. 'And what else?'

He ducks his head slightly, his gaze piercing. 'A chance to see your best friend again before it's too late.'

I bristle at his insinuation. 'Of course I'll see her again. When this is all over.'

His words are icy enough to send a chill down my spine. 'But what if you don't?'

I swallow, hating that I'm even considering his words. 'So, I would go with you. To the palace.' He nods slowly. 'And I would go see Paedyn while you see Hera?'

Another nod. 'As far as I know, they should be staying

in the same wing of the castle during the Trials. Though, annoyingly, I have no idea where that might be.'

'Which is why you want an Imperial uniform. So you can walk the halls freely while you search for the wing,' I breathe quietly, nodding in understanding.

'Exactly.' He extends a sooty hand, his lips tipping slightly in what might be considered a smile. 'Do we have a deal?'

My eyes flick up from his stained palm. 'You haven't asked me my name.'

He blows out a breath. 'Sorry, I was focused on more important details.' At the flat look on my face, he grumbles, 'By all means, please grace me with the knowledge of your name. I'm on the edge of my seat.'

I smile brightly. 'I'm Adena. Thank you very much for asking. And what is your name?'

After shooting me a sarcastic smile, he begrudgingly answers, 'Call me Mak.'

'Well, Mak —' I reach out to accept his calloused handshake — 'you now have yourself a partner.'

'Well, partner, we have to work quickly. There isn't much time before the Trials begin.'

CHAPTER 3

Makoto

'I'm assuming you're hungry, considering that you risked it all for a sticky bun.'

Her jaw drops into a comical look of shock, eyes anywhere but the busy street before us. Before she can even say anything, I'm wrapping an arm round her shoulders, rolling my eyes, and tugging her out of a rumbling cart's path.

Barely seeming to notice the inconvenience, the shocked expression doesn't budge from her face. 'How did you know I stole—' She cuts herself off, looking around nervously as though an Imperial may pounce at the mention of such a heinous crime. It's only when

she's deemed it safe that she whispers, 'How did you know I stole a sticky bun?'

'There's still honey on your hand,' I say dully. This has her tucking her arms behind her back, expression sheepish. 'And after seeing the Imperial chasing you, well, I'm brilliant enough to put two and two together.'

This all sounds very nonchalant, though the truth is nothing of the sort. I'd actually been watching her all morning and seen her pathetic attempt at theft. But I keep all of this to myself, of course, because I have a plan to carry out. A very stupid and slightly unhinged plan.

'Brilliant, huh?' she asks with a dubious arch of her brow.

'Self-proclaimed.'

She hums. 'I see.'

We walk in silence, surrounded only by the commotion of the street.

It's a blissful eight seconds.

'Do you have a job?'

I glance sidelong at her cheery expression. 'Self-employed.'

This time, she lasts all of six seconds before speaking again.

'Any hobbies?'

'Self-serving.' I meet her gaze before more sarcasm can slide off my tongue. 'Paired with the occasional self-loathing.'

Frustration tugs her lips into a frown, one she quickly smothers with one of her profoundly perky observations. 'Well, aren't you quite the conversationalist!'

I glance sidelong at her. 'Self-taught.'

The deep breath she takes is audible even over the constant bustle belonging to Loot. I almost smile. Because I'm a horrible person who doesn't believe that anyone could possibly be so happy. And maybe she truly is, though it's likely because she hasn't yet gotten to know me.

I might just crack her, seeing that I may be her worst nightmare – her opposite. And I'd be doing her a favor, really. Widening her range of emotions. Get her to embrace any other feeling besides permanent, unbearable perkiness.

Glancing over, I watch as she tilts her head towards the sky, skin glowing in the warm rays stroking her face. The light purple shirt she wears is falling down her arm, revealing a delicate collarbone and dark shoulder. My eyes trail over the black curls bouncing in time to each of her steps. Wind-blown bangs bleed into hazel eyes, bright with a sort of serenity that doesn't belong in the slums.

There is not a single cynical thought to deny the fact that she may be the most beautiful woman I've ever had the pleasure of laying eyes on. She's intimidatingly peaceful – a contradiction in itself. And I almost want to despise her for it. Because I fear there is a chance that I may begin to enjoy her.

'Soooo.' She draws out the word, giving me enough time to stop staring at her before I'm caught in the act. 'Where is it you're taking me?'

'Somewhere that will likely have you sneezing all over me.' Blandly, I add, 'So I'll be keeping my distance.'

She shrugs. 'So long as you're close enough to keep me company.'

This, unfortunately, piques my interest. 'I don't remember that being a part of the deal.'

She looks at me as though this is common knowledge. 'That's because it is a part of the deal that is knowing me.'

'Do you come with any other rules I should be made aware of?'

The expression she wears is the embodiment of a shrug. 'I don't like carrots. So none of those, please.' She taps a thin finger against her lips as though pondering something of far greater importance than our current topic. 'Oh, and I get scared very easily when I'm focused on my sewing, so don't sneak up on me or anything. I may poke you with a needle, so consider yourself warned.'

'Noted,' I sigh. 'Any other demands?'

A mischievous grin pulls at her lips. 'I expect a sticky bun every day. For my hard work, of course.'

I run my eyes over the length of her lean frame. 'Well, that's one way to get some meat on your bones.'

Turning my attention back towards the crowded street, I'm forced to dodge several carts along with the scrambling children weaving between them. Which, in turn, means I'm also guiding an alarmingly oblivious Adena.

'What are you looking at?' My tone is accusing. 'Because it certainly isn't the street in front of you.'

She smiles slightly at our surroundings. 'We clearly see the world quite differently.'

'See the world however you'd like, but at least watch your step while you do it.' I pause long enough to take in my own words. Then I'm glancing over at her with a surprised quirk of my brow. 'That was good advice. You should write that down.'

She laughs, though I'm certain it is at my expense. Nevertheless, I still get to enjoy the sound of it washing over me. 'Yes, very wise.'

I nod in the direction of a merchant and his cart of colorful fabric. 'How much do you need for the uniform? Couple of yards?'

I'm heading for the display of dizzying colors when a hand clamps round my bicep. 'What do you think you're doing?' she blurts, exasperated. 'I need to get your measurements before any fabric can be bought.'

'You can't be serious,' I say dryly. 'Why don't we get some now, and then—'

'We are doing this my way, Mak.' Her sudden sternness is almost startling. 'Or not at all.'

I raise a palm in mock surrender. 'Fine. I'm shocked you could stop smiling long enough to tell me off.'

She smiles at that, further proving my point. After several more steps down the street, I nod towards the alley on our right. 'This way.'

She follows me closely, like a too-short shadow attached to my heels. I lead her down the alley, stalling outside one of the many shop doors surrounded by crumbling brick. After fishing a key from a pocket decorating my leathers, so begins the routine of forcing the toothed iron into the lock.

It's only after me ramming my shoulder against the wood that the door swings open on squealing, rusty hinges. I brace an arm against it, gesturing for her to step inside. After she's offered me a quick smile, I watch her take in the entirety of my life with a single sweep of her eyes.

She paces around what can generously be described as a glorified shed. It's odd, watching someone take in the mess that is me.

She runs her fingers along the various tools and metal carelessly cast about the room. A thin layer of coal dust coats anything in the vicinity of the massive fireplace, staining half the room in grime.

My whole life takes place in this small amount of space. On one half of it all, I make a living as a blacksmith. But a messy bed lies on the other side, accompanied by several mismatching cabinets filled with whatever clothing and food I happen to have.

She seems to shy away from that intimate part of the room, though I watch her gaze linger on the crumpled covers of my bed. Her eyes stray back to the assortment of weapons lining the walls before poking at the large anvil beside the fireplace. 'You're a blacksmith.'

I cross my arms over my chest. 'How incredibly observant you are.'

Ignoring my comment, she asks, 'Who do you sell these weapons to?'

I shrug. 'Whoever is smart enough to want one.' I'm met with a questioning look, urging me to elaborate. 'Everyone in the slums should have a way to defend themselves. It's survival of the fittest.'

Her eyes are locked on the several shelves of weapons. 'I guess I've never seen Loot that way.' She frowns solemnly. 'It's always felt like a home.'

I swallow. 'Homes tend to hurt you the most.'

At that, she's quiet for a surprisingly long moment. That is, until she's not. 'So, you just hand someone whatever weapon they want?'

I lean against a wall, watching her take in my handiwork. 'Well, they typically ask me to teach them how to use whatever weapon they choose.'

She turns to face me with a shocked smile. 'And you help them?'

'Don't act so surprised.'

'Sorry,' she laughs defensively. 'It's just that, I thought you didn't have any goodness in your heart to give?'

'Well, not to you,' I scoff. 'I'm not wasting any of

my goodness on someone who clearly already has an abundance.'

She laughs again, and though that wasn't my intention, I'm not complaining about the outcome. 'I'll take that as a compliment.'

'Of course you will,' I mutter before pushing off the wall to stride towards her.

She tilts her head up to meet my gaze. 'Ready to get your measurements taken?'

'Do I have a choice?'

She beams. 'Nope!' Her eyes scan the room in search of something before she finally asks, 'Do you have a measuring tape?'

After tearing through my cluttered cabinets, I happen to find the rolled tape I stowed away. Adena makes quick work of unraveling it before I'm being ushered into the center of the room.

When she clears her throat, I look down at her in question. 'Um.' Her eyes shift uncomfortably. 'I'm going to need you to take your shirt off.' Before I can even open my mouth, she's rambling rapidly. 'See, I can't get a true measurement with all the pockets on your clothes. I mean, you can keep your pants on because the ones Imperials wear are loose as it is, so it's really just the shirt that needs to come off. Unless, you don't want to, of course—'

'This is not worth a ten-minute explanation.' I sigh while pulling the shirt from my body in one swift movement. It slides easily over my head, considering it's mostly made of a spandex material with a protective leather panel down the front.

I throw the shirt to the floor, watching her eyes follow the movement as she thoroughly avoids the sight of my bare chest. She squints down at the crumpled fabric before bending to run her fingers over it. 'The leather prevents most of the sparks from burning your skin?' When I nod in agreement to her observation, she adds softly, 'But the rest remains breathable enough to wear beside the fire.'

'And the pockets are just convenient for miscellaneous tools,' I add simply.

A small smile curves her lips. 'Reminds me of something I made for Pae. Except, the pockets were for stolen goods.'

We are quiet for several slow heartbeats.

'Alright, stretch out your arms for me, please.'

I reluctantly obey, standing before her with a bare chest and arms outstretched. She's quick to run the measuring tape along the length of each limb, jotting the measurements down on a scrap of paper she scavenged. Her eyes dart over my body, never staying too long on any patch of skin in particular. But I don't miss the bob of her throat, the brush of her fingers. Which are incredibly cold.

She smells of honey, of happiness incarnate. And it's entirely too distracting.

She then reaches her arms behind my back, encircling the tape round my chest. 'Don't mind me,' she mumbles awkwardly, her breath warm on my skin. After reading the measurement and proceeding to jot it down, she looks up with a comical look of concern. 'Well, someone is not eating their sticky buns.'

I give her a flat look. 'Well, someone has been eating – or stealing – them all before I can get one.'

'I certainly hope you're not accusing me.' Her eyes are wide, her frown impressive. 'Trust me, I would love to eat Loot out of their supply of sticky buns.' She looks me up and down, coming to a profound conclusion. 'Now it makes sense why you're so grumpy.'

'Ah, yes.' My voice is dull. 'My lack of ingested sticky buns. You've finally figured it out.'

But her attention is back on the crumpled paper in

her hand. 'Okay, get me five and a half yards of white fabric, just to be safe. You're much taller than my typical model – which would be Pae.' She shoves the parchment into my palm. 'Oh, and don't get the cheap fabric that unravels. This needs to look real, so get polyester.'

I blink as though that is question enough. 'And why aren't you coming with me?'

'Because,' she says slowly, her tone suggesting this is obvious, 'I have things to prepare. And a pre-sewing ritual, if you will.'

I suddenly feel a pounding headache coming on. 'Of course you do.' I quickly pull on my shirt before walking towards the door. 'Don't break anything.'

Her shout follows me out into the alley. 'Only if you get me a new needle!'

CHAPTER 4

Adena

I'm snooping.

A dangerous concoction of boredom and curiosity made me do it. After organizing my notes and calculating measurements, there was nothing left to do but poke around the messy collection of Mak's life.

I avoid the more personal side of the shop he lives in, though I study the bed and cabinets from afar. Oddly enough, it's his impressive assortment of weapons that intrigues me the most. I'm causing quite the commotion, clanking steel together and running my hands over everything in sight.

And then I gasp.

And that gasp is followed by a very unpleasant stinging.

Blood pools in my palm.

A crooked slice mars the center of my hand, spilling scarlet across my skin. The culprit lies on one of the many shelves straining beneath the weight of countless tools, its sharp blade buried harmlessly among them. I've barely held a dagger, let alone been sliced open by one. In fact, the most I've ever interacted with a blade has been when I hand Paedyn hers.

I'm considering dashing out the door and fleeing the kingdom. I haven't known Mak for long, but I do know that he will hardly be sympathetic. He'll likely mock and—

The door swings open, as though I've summoned him with my stupidity.

'I don't know what polyester is, but this shit better be that because it sure as hell wasn't cheap.'

I spin to face him, pushing my bloody hand behind my back. Tugging on a smile, I glance at the white bundle in his arms. Without warning, he's suddenly striding towards me, swallowing the space between us.

'Go on.' He nods down to the fabric. 'Make sure this is what you wanted.'

Swallowing, I pull the uninjured hand from behind my back while trying to ignore the biting sting of the other. Within one heartbeat, my fingers hover above the fabric. And in the next, his hand is clamped round my wrist, halting the movement.

'What did you do?' His voice is even, deliberate.

'Hmm?' I can feel my eyes widen with guilt. 'What are you talking about?'

A sigh. 'Let's not start lying to each other, hun. There's blood on your knuckle.'

My eyes fly down to my hand. 'Oh.'

'Yes, *oh.*' He reaches behind my back, brushing my hips in a way that sends a jolt down my body. After snatching my incriminating hand, his eyes widen slightly at the blood dripping from it. This may be the most emotion I've seen from him yet.

At the concern flitting across his face, I smile warmly. 'I'm fine, really. I just nicked myself with a blade. No need to worry.'

'It's a little late for that,' he says, eyes flicking up to meet mine. My heart warms at his sentiment, at this anticipated show of kindness. I knew he would come around, begin to show some sort of kindness for—

'Shoo, you're going to get blood on the fabric!'

My soft expression flattens into familiar dislike. 'And here I was, thinking you were worried about me.'

He strides over to his crumpled bed where he dumps the bundle of fabric, deeming it a safe distance from me and my staining hands. 'Well, maybe if I had to pay three silvers for you too, I'd be a little more worried.'

Plagues, I've never paid that much for fabric. Then again, I rarely pay for fabric, considering that Pae has her own methods of acquiring it for me.

He's suddenly towering over me once again, eyeing my bloody hand while I try my best not to wince in pain. An accusatory look lifts his eyebrows. 'Snooping?'

'Maybe a little,' I admit with a grumble.

He lifts my hand, his hold shockingly gentle as he examines it. 'How the hell did you manage to do this?'

'It's a gift, really,' I sigh. 'The only sharp object I trust myself with is a needle. And even that can be dangerous.'

'All right.' The hand he places on my back is light, feeling like the phantom of a touch, as though I'm simply imagining it. 'Let's get you cleaned up. Out of the goodness of my heart, I might add.'

I glance over my shoulder at him. 'I thought you weren't giving any of that to me?'

'You've forced my hand.'

He guides me towards the intimate half of the room I haven't dared venture into. The half that feels too personal for my prodding.

His disheveled bed looms closer with each step, along with a string of makeshift cabinets lining the opposite wall. I stop before I collide with the counter, turning to give him a questioning look.

That's when my feet leave the ground.

I gasp, possibly squeal, when he lifts me onto the surface with ease.

The gawk I give him is met with a dry look. 'I'd rather you not bloody my counter while trying to get up here.'

His hands are still firm on my hips while my breath is still lodged in my throat. I attempt to blink the bewildered look from my face. 'Right. Yeah, of course.'

He manages to pull most of his hair into a strap, though several pieces fall around his face, some slipping down his neck.

My face flushes at the sight, as though seeing his bare chest earlier was less of a distraction than the sight of his messy hair.

Grabbing my injured hand in one of his own, he uses

the other to lift a canteen of water off the counter beside me. After unscrewing the cap with his teeth, he tips the liquid out onto my palm. Cool water meets my bloody gash, stinging as it seeps into the slice now drowning in crimson swirls.

I bite my lip in an attempt to ward off the tears welling in my eyes. I've never been much good with pain. Never needed to be. But I refuse to be ashamed of my softness. Gentleness is the strength that fragility lacks.

'I'm sorry,' he starts quietly, 'that something of mine has already wounded you.'

I shrug slightly. 'And I'm sorry about your knife.'

His eyes flick up to mine. 'And why is that?'

'Because I got it all bloody.'

I happen to look up in time, witnessing the beautiful accident that has happened.

I've made him smile.

At first, it looks as though he's trying to fight it, like a habit that has been long broken. And then it's all white teeth and crinkled eyes; smile lines and deep chuckles.

It transforms his face, painting his features in warmth. His icy expression melts, revealing soft accents and a stunning smile. The thin scar gracing his lips stretches into something much softer, something far less intimidating.

This is the face of a boy who hasn't yet been hardened by life itself.

'So, he does smile!' I say, wearing one of my own.

And then I immediately regret opening my mouth. It's as though the words have smothered the spark that lit up his face. The stony expression suddenly seeps back in. 'Don't go getting used to it.'

'Yes, Plagues forbid anyone thought you were actually happy once in a while,' I mumble teasingly before suddenly deciding on something. 'I'm determined to make you smile again.'

I watch him dab lightly at the wound, staining the towel he uses with each swipe. My knee bobs anxiously atop the counter, awaiting his response while rattling the now empty canteen beside me. He glances down at the commotion I'm causing, then back at his hands still tending to my own. With every other limb occupied, he simply leans towards me, pressing his body against my bouncing appendage.

The weight of his hip burns through every layer of clothing, every rational thought, every fiber of my frenzied being. My knee stills beneath the pressure he applies, my heart doing the same at the sheer closeness of him.

He manages to lean in further, murmuring, 'You'll have to earn it, honey.'

I'm not sure what's gotten into me, but it's suddenly difficult to swallow the lump growing in my throat at the sound of his deep voice. 'And why is that?'

'Because I'm hardly deserving of them myself.'

It's clear that he doesn't wish to elaborate on his vagueness. We eye each other for a long moment before he begins digging around in a cabinet, pulling an unraveling roll of medical cloth from its depths. Tearing it with the teeth I'll likely never get to glimpse again, he begins thoroughly wrapping the width of my palm.

'There,' he says blandly, stepping back to admire his work. 'No chance of you bloodying my fabric now.'

'Might look more realistic that way,' I offer with a tilt of my head. 'Have you seen how stained most Imperial uniforms are?'

'Dammit, Adena,' he huffs. 'Maybe mention that before I heroically tend to your wound.'

CHAPTER 5

Makoto

Her head bobs dangerously close to the sharp needle slipping from between her fingers.

She startles, swallowing her gasp as she blinks awake. Tired eyes meet mine from where I'm leaning over my work table, sketching a new knife design.

I turn back to my work, unsurprised by anything she does at this point. 'You're going to stab yourself again.'

'I've worked through the night before,' she says defensively, though actively fighting a yawn. 'I'll be fine.'

'This time it'll be your eye.' I sigh. 'Maybe your

throat. Definitely a couple fingers.'

'I'm not going to stab anything, Mak.' She breathes my name and I'm surprised by the affect it has on me from a person so pretty.

I straighten, striding towards her. 'No, you will not.' She sputters when I pluck the needle from her fingers. 'Because I am taking this for the night.'

'No, there's so much left to do,' she argues, gesturing to the assortment of pinned fabric. 'I've barely begun the stitching, and don't even get me started on how long the paneling will take on the—'

'You've been working for two full days now.' I cross my arms over my chest. 'And I've heard enough words for today. I can't imagine how exhausted you must be after speaking them all.'

Her dull look could rival one of the many in my arsenal. 'Is this you kicking me out for the night?'

I flash her a mocking smile. 'Don't let the door hit you on the way out.'

'Fine.' She stands, staring up at me sternly. It's comically endearing. 'Hopefully some sleep will make you less grumpy for me tomorrow.'

'Did that work for me last night?'

'Clearly not, but I won't lose hope. Yet.'

'Whatever helps you sleep better tonight,' I say pleasantly.

She brushes past me, walking swiftly towards the door. Then, without warning, she spins on her heel. 'I'll be here, bright and early.'

'Oh, you certainly were this morning,' I mutter.

She turns back to the door.

I sigh when her head whips back around.

'And I expect to be greeted with a smile and a sticky bun.' She nods curtly, as though finalizing this demand.

I cross my arms. 'I thought we were done with the demands, hun?'

'Get me my sticky bun, and we will be.'

With that, she's sealed from view when the wooden door swings shut behind her with a squeal.

It's only then that I take my first deep breath since meeting her.

She is an intoxicating sort of exhausting, like running until you've lost your breath but enjoying the feeling all the while. And I feel as though I've been sprinting for days.

Even worse, I fear that I am, in fact, beginning to enjoy her.

What a terrifying realization, to admit one's admiration for another.

I run my hands through the strands of hair falling around my face, sighing as I make my way over to the disheveled bed I so desperately want to fall face-first into. Instead, I sit on the edge of it, lost in thoughts I'd rather not entertain. Thoughts of a girl I've only just met, of all things. How very pathetically poetic.

Shaking myself from a stupor of inevitable self-destruction, I stand to begin my nightly routine. This consists of first peeling the coal-stained clothes from my body. Once that task is complete, I slip off the partially leathered pants still hugging my legs. And after rummaging through one of the many crooked cabinets in my boxers alone, I manage to find a thin pair of pants to pull on.

This all happens in a timely manner, as routines typically do. Because next, I'm wetting a cloth to wipe the soot from my skin. In all honesty – a relatively foreign concept – I tend to keel over on my work table at this hour, dead asleep. But tonight, the interruption in my routine has ensured that my mind is plenty awake to actually finish it for once.

Soot clings to the damp cloth I drag across my skin,

each swipe revealing the scars beneath.

That is when the pounding at my door begins.

And, Plagues, it doesn't stop until I swing it open.

It's her I see standing before me. Though, perhaps a version I never thought I'd witness. Her face is splotchy, striped with tears that leak from the hazel eyes above. Every inch of her is shaking, quaking beneath the fear smothering her frail form.

Panic clogs her throat, leaving only actions to speak on her behalf. She falls into me, wrapping thin arms round my bare waist before pressing a tear-stained face into my skin.

I hesitate, feeling uncertainty stiffen my body. It seems to pass at the acknowledgment of it, as though only remaining long enough for me to recognize these newfound emotions she's instilled in me. Because uncertainty implies that I care enough to question how I should act.

With that horrifying realization, my arms fold round her, pulling her tightly against my chest. She sniffles against me, splattering my skin with an assortment of liquids I'd rather not consider at the moment.

'I-I'm sorry,' she whispers, choking on the words. 'I had nowhere else to go.'

My hand tilts her face up towards mine, allowing me full view of her distraught expression. 'What happened? What's going on?'

Another sniff. 'I was on my way to the F-Fort, and there was this group of men in the alley.' My blood begins to boil before she's even finished her sentence. 'They started saying . . . things. And then they were f-following me and—' Her eyes well with angry tears. 'I started running. I-I didn't know what to do—'

'Shh.' I run a hand down the length of her curls, feeling a hiccup jostle her body. 'You did the right thing. Run to me. Always run to me.'

Except that I won't be here much longer. If everything goes according to plan.

I say none of that, of course, in an effort to conceal my cowardliness. She blinks up at me, tears clinging to her thick lashes. 'Did I wake you? I'm sorry, I should have—'

'Kicked their asses?' I finish with a sigh. 'Yes, but you don't know how to do that, do you?'

She shakes her head, sniffling with the movement. 'Pae was always there to kick . . . asses for me.'

She hesitates at the profanity, as though considering if this situation warrants it. Her internal dilemma almost makes me smile.

'Yes, well, she's not here anymore,' I say slowly. 'So, maybe it's time for you to learn for yourself.'

She steps out of my hold, a look of uncertainty on her face. 'You see, I'm really more of a lover than a fighter.'

'Yes, I've gathered that.' My words are much softer than anticipated, as though she's somehow coaxed the compassion out of me. She turns away, hiding her face in the shadow I'm casting over her. 'Look at me.' Again, each word is soft enough to comfort, but stern enough to steal her attention. Her head tilts back towards me. 'Are you all right?'

She nods vigorously. 'I am now.'

'Good.' I step aside, offering the room to her. 'Because it looks like you'll be sleeping here until further notice.'

'Oh, no, I couldn't—'

'You can. And you will.'

'No, really, it's—'

'Extremely generous, I'm aware,' I finish for her.

Wiping a stray tear from her cheek, she straightens with determination. 'Fine. Only if you promise to spend a night in the Fort.'

I nod curtly. 'Sure.'

'Shake on it,' she insists, shoving her uninjured hand at me.

'You really think that is what will make me keep my promise?'

She wiggles her fingers despite my words, and I shake her soft hand if only so we can move on from this conversation.

'Okay. It's settled, then.' She sniffs again before thoroughly clearing her face of any fallen tears. Then her gaze lands expectantly on me.

'Right,' I say, less than enthusiastically. 'Take the bed.'

She looks bashfully at the crumpled sheets. 'Oh, I'm used to sleeping on the ground anyway, so I'll just—'

'Accept my continued generosity?' She opens her mouth, but it's my voice that fills the room. 'Great. Take the bed.'

Her hands are suddenly planted firmly on her hips. 'Could I get a please with that demand?'

'Aw, look who's finally standing up for themselves.' I tap my finger against her nose. 'But no.'

Huffing bangs out of her eyes, she walks hesitantly towards the bed. After a long moment of contemplation, she sits stiffly on the edge of it.

Standing over her, I begin pulling at one of the wrinkled blankets she's currently sitting on. She all but tips over, sputtering. In response to her objection, I spread the soft fabric on the floor beside the bed. 'Surely you can sacrifice a single blanket for me.'

'Surely you could have asked me to stand up,' she mumbles with a forced smile.

'Surely you know there is no fun in that.'

Her gaze prickles my skin as I crumple clothing into a makeshift pillow. I struggle to ignore the feel of it, the look on her face. Even in the midst of crying, she managed to glow, as though each tear was a drop of sunlight.

'You missed a spot.'

My head lifts at the sound of her voice. I raise my eyebrows in question. 'The coal dust,' she clarifies. 'There's still some on your elbow.'

'Do stay away, then.' I frown. 'I'd rather not be sneezed on again.'

She smiles, snatching the damp cloth from the counter sitting opposite the bed. 'Oh, don't be ridiculous.' Grabbing my arm, she attempts to tug me towards her. And, begrudgingly, I allow it.

She hesitates slightly before swiping the cloth across

my arm. The fabric is rough against my skin, though her touch is unsurprisingly gentle. 'I'm far from fragile.' I say this in response to each of her tender touches.

'I know,' she says softly. 'There is quite the difference between fragility and delicacy.'

These words are nothing like the hundreds of bubbly ones prior. These words are deliberate, insightful in a way that only she is. 'So, you think I'm delicate?'

She tilts her head in question. 'Don't you want to be handled with care?'

This leaves me speechless.

It's only when she sets the stained cloth down that I clear my throat, making my first sound in a multitude of moments. I watch her sink back onto the mattress, burrowing into the blankets beneath her.

That is when I begin striding towards the door, shoving daggers into the band of my pants.

I can hear the concern in her voice. 'Where are you going?'

The door swings open. 'To find them.'

CHAPTER 6

Adena

I wake to the smell of sticky buns.

Just as I have every morning after Mak went to find the men who chased me into his arms. Though, I'm not entirely sure what came of his hunt – and I'm beginning to fear I may not want to know.

The night still haunts me, as does the look on Mak's face when he went to look for the vile group. The things they were saying, the sound of their footsteps pounding behind me – I hope to never be so frightened again.

My eyes flutter open in time to watch him plop a plate onto my stomach, occupied by honey-drenched dough that glistens in the dull light. I sit up, stretching

with my usual smiling yawn. 'Day three of breakfast in bed? I'm so spoiled.'

'Yes, very.' He says this dryly, as he does most things. 'Another day, another demand.'

I nod towards the sticky bun awaiting him on the work table. 'At least this demand benefits the both of us.'

'Well, it sure as hell doesn't benefit me financially,' he grumbles. 'You're getting to be expensive.'

Unfolding myself from the cocoon of blankets, I get to my feet with a groan. The blue sweater hanging from my shoulder swaddles me in warmth and, more distractingly, his scent. He smells of something akin to fire – not smoky, per se, but similarly bold and lingering. Like a weapon incarnate, leathery and lethal.

He'd thrown the sweater at my head two nights ago after likening my chattering teeth to the incessant hammering of steel – or something equally as dramatic.

Nevertheless, I burrow my chin into the worn threads, finding comfort in the fraying collar. Or perhaps it's something far more symbolic that soothes me. Perhaps it's him.

How odd, considering that he may be the least soothing person I've ever encountered. But these past few days have felt particularly peaceful with him by my side.

I talk. He listens. He has somehow managed to keep my worries about Pae at bay.

Well, I can never be entirely sure if he's listening or not. A common misconception about me is that it's always easy to talk. But, truly, it depends on who is listening. And though I can never be sure that he's doing just that, I still find it incredibly easy to spew my thoughts to him.

'What are you working on?' I peek over his shoulder, peering down at the scraps of metal littering the table.

He throws me one of those glances, the type that encompasses every dry emotion in his being. 'Nothing that concerns what you are supposed to be working on.'

'Oh, come on!' I take another bite of sticky bun before circling him. 'Your uniform is coming along just fine.' He opens his mouth, stretching the scar gracing his lips. I hurry to add, 'And it will be done in time for us to pay our visit to the castle.'

He pushes a hand through his hair, revealing that streak of silver and reminding me once again of Pae's absence. 'So, it will be done in three days, then?'

'Yes, yes,' I assure enthusiastically. 'You have such little faith in me, Mak.'

'Rightfully so,' he counters. 'Need I remind you of the tears that were shed over a button last night?'

'Buttons are the bane of my existence,' I say simply. 'That was the only appropriate response.'

'Naturally.' His sarcasm hardly fazes me as I nod towards his work in question. With a sigh, he reluctantly says, 'I'm testing some knife designs. This one,' he lifts a thin blade from the table, 'flips open into two knives.' He demonstrates, fitting his finger into the metal loop at the top before spinning it into his palm. Sure enough, there's a soft click before another blade appears on the opposite end.

'And this one?' I ask, pointing at one of the several knives lying harmlessly on the wood.

He pushes my hand away, giving me a look. 'Your limbs are no longer allowed anywhere near my weapons.'

I attempt to hide my smile and nod at the knife instead, urging him to continue.

'These four actually combine into one.' With that, he begins assembling the blades, hooking their handles together to create a deadly star of sorts.

My heart stops when he throws the contraption at the far wall, forcing a gasp from my lips. The steel manages to slip between the crumbling bricks, sinking deep into the wall.

I blink in awe as my heart pounds back to life. 'That was . . . magnificent.'

He allows himself a dry chuckle. 'I didn't think you'd enjoy these sorts of things.'

I cross my arms. 'Just because I'm a lover, doesn't mean I can't admire the fighters.'

He strides over to the wall, pulling the knife out with a grunt. 'That's right. I have yet to make a fighter out of you.'

I snort. 'Trust me, Pae has tried. She used to beg me to carry a knife but . . .' I trail off at the sudden lack of space between us. His long strides have led him straight to me, his body so close that I can smell the leather clinging to his clothing.

I open my mouth to spew something that will ease my nerves – as I typically do – but it's his voice I hear.

'Now,' he says slowly, his tone low, 'what would you do if I held this blade to your stomach?'

I laugh lightly. 'Well, you would never do that, so I haven't exactly thought of—'

He grazes the blade against my ribs.

He leans in, whispering in a way that has my face

heating. 'You think too highly of me, hun.'

I swallow. 'This is absurd. I will never find myself in this situation—'

'As long as you live in the slums,' he pauses, his gaze flicking slowly over me, 'you will most definitely find yourself in this situation.'

'Now, tell me what you would do.'

I tap a finger against my lips. 'Well, I would first try to reason with them. Politely, of course.'

'Plagues.' Pinching the bridge of his nose between calloused fingers, he shakes his head. 'You may actually be hopeless.'

He drops the knife, allowing me to finally take a full breath. When he raises his palms in front of me, I raise my eyebrows in question. 'Come on, show me a punch.'

'You want me to punch your hands? That seems a little painful.'

'You'll be fine,' he sighs.

'I meant for you.'

That almost earns me a smile. 'I think I can handle it.'

I straighten, balling my hands into tight fists. My knuckles meet his palm, and I beam up at him. 'There. How was that?'

'As terrible as predicted,' he says simply. When his hands find my hips, I startle at the firm feel of them. 'This,' he twists my hips with little effort, 'is how it should feel when you throw a punch.'

I almost laugh. At this moment, all I feel is the grip of his hands on my hips. I seem to be numb to everything but the feel of him.

I hadn't realized he was speaking until one of his palms slips into the small of my back. '. . . twist with your arm to throw all your weight behind it. Straighten your back and engage your core. Your whole body throws the punch, not just your arm.'

He steps behind me then, trailing his fingers around my waist as he does so. I can hardly suppress my shiver, at this foreign feeling. Tucking his head close to mine, he breathes, 'Try again. I'll guide you.'

I swallow, mostly my pride but also my sudden wave of nerves. When my arm thrusts forward, he pivots my hips, moving in time with the swing. The heat of his body presses against my back, and I'm suddenly breathing far too hard for a single punch.

'How'd that feel?' he murmurs.

I vaguely wonder if he can detect my heart pounding through the back he's pressed against. I'm not used to being touched – not like this at least. This feels like the type of intimacy I've only ever dreamed of; the type you fall asleep fantasizing about.

But here he is, breath on my neck and calloused hands cupping my hips. I can't help but memorize the moment, study the feelings he stirs inside of me. Feelings for someone so annoyingly aggravating. Someone so opposite my very being.

I clear my throat.

It's completely ridiculous, really. I've only known this man a handful of days and am already absurdly affected by his every move. It truly is a curse to feel so deeply, to so daringly deem someone worthy of my affection.

Mama always did say I was much too eager for my own good. My impatience ensures that I won't gradually fall for someone. Instead, I lose my balance, tripping until I face-plant into inevitable failure.

'Again, Dena.'

I think I've forgotten how to breathe.

Dena.

The usual indifference he wears falters when I whip my head round to face him. I can see the realization in the way his brown eyes widen in time with my own, in the feel of his body tensing against mine.

No one but Pae has ever cared enough to call me by anything but my given name. Until now, that is.

The name itself feels like a caress, stilling my pounding heart as though he's run figurative fingers down it. Warmth floods my body at the sound, at the sheer implication of the word. Because it was formed by familiarity.

Nicknames blossom between acquaintance and something more. Though, I'm not sure where we stand on that spectrum. Or perhaps I'm being completely absurd and am completely overthinking everything—

I'm suddenly being spun around with firm hands that have found their way to my waist. My lower back bumps into the wooden table, trapping me against the distracting density of him.

He gives me that look. The one where he tilts his head down with a dull twist of his lips. 'I hope it was your fighting technique you were daydreaming about.'

I tilt my head up, apparently unable to keep my eyes from tracing the scar cutting his lips. 'What else would possibly be on my mind?' I smile, each word breathy.

'You tell me.' He leans in, bracing his hands on the table either side of me. I feel his arms brushing my sides and curse myself for the lack of self-restraint I possess.

'You're looking far more fidgety than normal. I can't say I enjoy it.'

I clear my throat before pasting a smile onto my face, pretending as though I'm not suddenly thinking of him as something more than a begrudging partner. 'Guess I just can't contain my excitement for this very enjoyable training you're forcing me to do!'

He blinks, shaking his head in disbelief. 'All right, remind me to teach you how to lie next.' I nod before his hands find my hips once again, sending a shock all the way down to my toes. 'Now, keep swinging until I'm satisfied you could hit me.'

I punch. His fingers grip my hips.

I punch. His hand flattens against my back.

I punch. His lips almost form a smile.

And so begins my doomed trip into Mak.

CHAPTER 7

Makoto

'Stop laughing. This isn't funny.'

She giggles again in a way that makes it hard to stay angry – even for me. But when the needle's point finds the tip of my finger once again, I toss the fabric aside with a huff.

'Oh, please, don't give up.' The look of disappointment on her face almost makes me reconsider. 'Look at how far you've come!'

'What, you mean the twelve crooked stitches?' I lift the scrap of fabric for proof. 'Yeah, I'm clearly a prodigy.'

She presses her lips together, fighting an aggravating smile. It's become increasingly less so over the past

couple of days. But I'd rather not think on that at the moment.

'Look, it's only fair that you try my thing after putting me through yours yesterday,' she states while stitching a pant seam with ease. 'For hours.'

'Don't be dramatic.' I sigh. 'Besides, at least my *thing* will help you defend yourself.'

Adena points her needle at me. 'You haven't seen me wield this thing yet.'

My eyes skim over the scraps of loose fabric beside the uniform she's still assembling. 'Is that not what you're doing now?'

She ponders this for a moment. 'I suppose it is.'

'I'll be truly impressed when you have me looking like an Imperial in two days.'

'I know, I know,' she huffs. 'Only two more days until our fun little mission to the castle.'

I shake my head. 'Don't call it that.'

'I am so excited to see Pae,' she practically squeals, content to ignore me. 'All that's left to do is line the suit to mimic the padding that the Imperials have. Oh, and cut the leather for your mask.'

'Great.' I take a deep breath, relieved. 'And you remember the plan, correct?' Despite her incessant nodding, I figure it's best to remind her. 'We'll leave early in the evening, giving us over an hour to make it to the Arena. There, we will—'

'Sneak up the path to the east wing of the castle before phasing through the walls and past the guards.' She smiles smugly. 'See, I told you I remembered.'

'Incredibly impressive,' I counter dryly. 'Now, we will stick together and phase into rooms when necessary—'

'Wait, what am I wearing on our little mission?'

I pinch the bridge of my nose, feeling a headache beginning to pound. 'Please. Don't call it a—'

'I could dress up like a maid!' She taps a finger against her lips in thought. 'Though I'm not entirely sure what it is they wear . . .'

'Just tie an apron round your waist,' I say dismissively. 'It will be dark anyway. It's unlikely anyone will see you.'

'Perfect.' Then she nods to the pathetic piece of shit she's forced me to work on. 'Now, go on. You've got more stitches to do.'

'You can't be serious.'

She laughs lightly. 'You should have seen my stitches when Mama first tried to teach me. It was a disaster.'

Her voice softens before trailing off at the mention of a life I know nothing about.

'You don't talk about her,' I say quietly. 'In fact, you don't talk about anyone who isn't Pae.'

She shrugs as though the past that brought her to this present is of little importance. 'There's not much to say. Besides –' she glances up at me with those wide, hazel eyes – 'you never talk about Hera.'

'There's not much to say,' I counter.

'That's odd.' Her voice is nonchalant, but her piercing gaze is anything but. 'I figured she was pretty important for you to go through all this trouble to see her one last time.'

Right. I'm supposed to be seeing her one last time. Not attempting anything treasonous.

I let out an exasperated sound. 'Your curiosity is exhausting, honey.'

'Speaking of,' she says enthusiastically while wearing a frown, 'I'm afraid I don't know much about you. Apart from your measurements – which I now have memorized, by the way.'

'I hope you know that I find that slightly unnerving—'

'Well, if you won't tell me about Hera,' she cuts

in, looking slightly ruffled by my withholding of information, 'tell me something else.'

'I just did.' A pause. 'Your curiosity exhausts me.'

Rolling those hazel eyes, she pushes on valiantly. 'What about your family?'

I almost muster a laugh. 'Oh, just the friendliest bunch. You would love them.'

Apparently, she doesn't sense the added sarcasm I've slipped into the syllables of each word. 'Oh, how wonderful! I would love to meet them one day.' Her face flushes suddenly before she's adding, 'I mean, if we still see each other after all of this.'

And there it is, that pang of guilt. Guilt at the thought of leaving her, of giving her hope of something that will inevitably fail. Because nothing good could come of us. Hera was the only weakness I allowed myself to have, the only person I let get close enough. And look what it got her – a death sentence.

Tragedy follows me everywhere I go, and I'm not worthy of becoming her demise. Adena deserves a fairytale fate, a life worthy of her light. And that means I should stay as far away from it as possible.

I *should*.

'I don't think we should see each other after all this.'

Her eyes fly up from the path of stitches she's laying along the pant leg. 'W-Why?'

I shrug with a nonchalance I'm pretending to portray. 'Because my unpleasantness may rub off on you.'

She lifts her chin, wearing that bright smile of hers. 'I think you're just worried that I'll make you nicer.'

I frown. 'That would be unfortunate. I have a reputation to uphold.'

Her eyes are back on the uniform draped in her lap. 'How did you learn to fight?'

My throat tightens, forcing me to swallow before saying, 'Self-taught.'

Persistence has her pressing for elaboration. 'Why? Because you wanted to learn how to use the weapons you were making?'

Because I was afraid.

'My father was a blacksmith.' My voice is dull. 'I learned everything I know from watching him. Most of the fighting, too.'

Before she can interrogate me further, I order, 'All right, show me that you remember all of my hard work yesterday.'

'*Your* hard work?' She stands with a groan. 'I'm the one who punched the air a couple dozen times.'

'Yes, and it caused me a great amount of pain to watch.'

I place a hand on her back, feeling the sway of her hips with each step. Attempting to ignore that distraction, I guide her towards a padded wall, once concealed by a cluttered shelf of weapons.

I gesture towards the dusty mat I rigged up years ago. 'No more punching air.'

'Oh, perfect,' she says less than enthusiastically. 'Now I get to punch something that will actually hurt.'

'I've punched this many a time, hun. It won't hit back, I assure you.'

I take my usual position behind her, and she swings at the pad far softer than I've taught her. 'Come on, Dena. You won't hurt it.'

And there I go again. Claiming her.

The name slips past my lips for the second time, and once again, I'm regretting it. Regretting the familiarity forming between us.

After clearing her throat, she attempts another jab. I twist her hip in time with the movement, feeling my palm fit around her frame.

Curly hair continually whips me in the face, smelling of its usual honey. But I don't dare complain at her closeness, for fear of her shying away.

'I wonder what Pae will be wearing to the ball.' Adena sighs, slowing her punches. 'They better put her in something that won't wash her out with that silver hair of hers. And she absolutely refuses to wear anything frilly or—'

'Focus, Adena.'

It was an effort to ensure it wasn't my nickname for her that escaped my lips.

'I mean, it's hard enough to get her into anything that isn't that vest I made her,' she continues as though I hadn't even opened my mouth.

I sigh, desperate for a change of subject. 'Is Pae your only family, or simply your only topic of conversation?'

She throws a look over her shoulder, subtle annoyance sketched into her features. 'It was just my mama and me before she died.'

My hand tightens slightly on her hip before she takes another swing, this one much stronger than before. 'I . . .' Sentiments have never come easy to me. 'I'm sorry. I didn't know.'

She shrugs, and my hand glides towards the movement. The sound of her sucking in a breath threatens to make me smile, but I hold my composure as I run a palm over the length of her stiff shoulder. I can feel the shudder of her body beneath my skin.

'It's okay,' she breathes, her voice shaky. 'She was sick. There was nothing the Healer could do.'

'And you've been living on the streets ever since?' I ask quietly.

'Five years now.' She nods in that reminiscent way. 'Five years in the Fort with Pae.' That's when she whips around, slapping curls across my face. 'Oh, I still have to show you the Fort! You promised you'd spend the night there.'

I push her jabbing finger out of my face. 'Did I? I don't recall.'

Now she's crossed thin arms over her chest. 'Don't you lie to me, Mak—' She stumbles over her scrutiny before fixing me with a defiant look. 'How am I supposed to properly scold you if I don't know your full name?'

'Good.' I brush a curl from her eyes so she can see me clearly as I say, 'Let's keep it that way.'

The sound that comes from her throat is comparable to a frustrated groan. 'Am I allowed to know anything about you?'

'Of course.' I nod towards the uniform stretched out on the floor. 'My measurements.'

Her eyes shut slowly, fluttering dark lashes against

soft cheeks. It's comical, watching the frustration flash across her features. But she smothers it quickly with a smile in that typical Adena way. 'Fine.' This smile has a sort of bite to it. 'Then you don't get to know anything about me either.'

I nod slowly, if only so I can conceal my slight smile with the strands of hair falling around my face.

Oh, I already know far too much.

CHAPTER 8

Adena

'Can I open my eyes now? Are you decent?'

There's a rustle of fabric followed by a dry answer. 'I'm clothed, if that's what you're asking.'

I peek open an eye that lands on the crisp white pants hanging from his hips—

My lips press together.

His hips are still bare.

He's standing there with only half a uniform on, leaving his chest exposed and my eyes wide. My gaze skims over the scattered scars marring his skin before I finally muster the strength to look away. A handful of days ago, his bare chest would be less of an intriguing sight, but now . . .

Now, I'm horribly enthralled by all of him.

'What?' he asks with a scrutinizing stare. 'Don't act like I'm the only man you've seen without a shirt on.'

'Hmm?' My cheeks burn. 'Right.'

He stills, eyes narrowing. 'I'm not, am I?'

'No,' I blurt defensively, 'there are plenty of men who walk around Loot without a shirt on . . .'

'Right.' He nods slowly. 'And do you always stare at them this intensely?'

I didn't think my face could get any hotter. 'Whatever. Hurry up, I have places to be.' I stumble through my words before turning round to curse myself away from his prying eyes.

'Is that so?' His tone is mocking. 'And where are you off to besides the palace tonight?'

'In case you've forgotten,' I state with satisfaction, 'I have a business to run.'

'Ah, yes.' I glance back in time to catch him tugging the top half of his uniform over the messy waves falling around his face. 'You have clothes to sell. Now even those living in the slums can starve in style.'

I give him the new look I've developed – a cross between unimpressed and slightly amused. 'Well, when you put it like that . . .'

He scoffs before raising his arms, surveying the length of my handiwork. 'Do I look the part? In the dark, at the very least.'

I take a few slow steps toward his white-clad figure, eyeing every seam and panel along the fabric. Then I'm clapping my hands together, squealing slightly. 'It's perfect! You look more menacing than usual.'

His lips twitch. 'It's about time you gave me a compliment.'

'Oh, wait, one more thing.' I snatch the leather mask from the dusty work table. Stepping close enough to smell the starch I've doused his uniform in – for authenticity, of course – I look up into dark eyes already pinned on me.

I'm acutely aware that we are sharing the same air as I reach up to fasten the mask over his eyes and nose. The feel of his gaze roaming over my face has my palms growing sweaty. But I continue my admiration of his own features, following the curve of his cheekbones beneath the mask, the straight bridge of his nose in the center. When my gaze glides over the scar decorating his lips, I'm forced to fight the urge to run my finger over it.

'Still menacing?' he murmurs, his face hovering over mine.

'More than ever,' I assure breathlessly.

We watch each other for several shaky breaths before he clears his throat. 'Don't you have places to be? A particular blue shirt to sell?'

At the mention of my creation he so ruthlessly criticized, I gain the strength to take a step away from him. 'Why, yes, I do. And if it doesn't sell, I know exactly what I'll be wearing on our little mission.'

He shakes his head in disbelief, crossing large arms over his chest. 'You know, you are far more conniving than you look.'

I tip my chin up. 'And how exactly do I look?'

'Sweet. Unassuming. Pretty enough to get away with wearing that horribly blue shirt.'

My throat is dry, but I attempt a swallow anyway. He's looking down at me in the same way I do my stitching. Admiration lights his eyes even while he searches for any sort of fault to focus on. As though he aches for a reason to rip at the seams of what it is that has slowly tethered us together.

'Then wear it I shall,' I reassure him.

After fumbling for the door – an action typically associated with when his eyes linger over me – I hurry out onto the alleyway.

Sun dapples my face, freckling my nose with warmth as I hurry down Loot. I find the Fort thankfully untouched, seeing that to the untrained eye it is, in fact, a pile of garbage. I'm reminded of my decision to redecorate for Pae when she returns and add the task to my mental list of chores.

Lifting one of the many rugs, I find clothing buried beneath, belonging to the bundle I'd thrown into the alley during my attempted robbery. After meeting Mak, I came back to properly collect and dust off my work before ensuring every scrap of fabric was hidden beneath the many layers of the Fort.

Once I've gathered the bundle of clothing in my arms, I set off towards the corner I've neglected for nearly two weeks now. But after tonight, I will no longer be fed for free or cozied up beneath the cover of his sheets – not that I wouldn't want that to continue. But Mak has made it very clear that I shouldn't be seeing him after our mission. Though, I have yet to find a good reason as to why.

He makes me happy, for whatever absurdly odd reason. He's not exactly a ray of sunshine, but perhaps something equivalent to moonlight. Mysterious and unnerving. Equally as beautiful, yet, soft enough to stare at.

With thoughts of Mak consuming whatever rationality I had left, I hurry down the bustling street. I'm nearly at my corner now and have yet to drop a single item of clothing. This is something I hope will become a regular occurrence. With that goal in mind, I hug the mass of fabric tighter as I hurry towards the mouth of my usual alley.

Most merchants have carts to sell from. I have other methods.

Years ago, Pae and I fastened a long wire across the opening of this alley, and I am shocked to find the rusty nails still holding. While balancing the bundle of clothing in my arms, I begin draping them across the line to display my handiwork. It makes for a makeshift sort of banner, colorful enough to draw attention.

Once each piece is arranged to my liking, I plop down beneath the display and fight the urge to pick at my nails in boredom. Deciding to spend my time wisely, I begin fiddling with the bits of leftover leather from Mak's uniform.

The display of his knife collection comes to mind as I run my thumb over the smooth material. He has no way to carry them on him without fear of being stabbed by protruding blades.

That's when an idea begins to form. Patterns and measurements are suddenly swirling behind my closed eyelids, aligning into a tangible design. I begin tearing fabric and pinning corners, watching my idea come to life.

That's when my stomach grumbles at me, the sound a reminder of the little money I have. And with that in mind, I smile brightly at each person who passes, as if that is enough to persuade them to buy something.

And just when I'm starting to think my attempts are scaring customers away, a man strolls towards me.

I stand, drape my project over the wire, and greet him with what I hope is a slightly less desperate smile. I watch him grow closer, watch fuzzy features become more familiar with every step.

I know this man. His is one of the faces I see when shutting my eyes before bed.

This is one of the men that followed me.

'Hello, pretty,' he croons, closing the distance between us. 'You're even nicer to look at in the daytime.'

My eyes shift nervously, glancing at the passing people. With what may be a false sense of security, I attempt to keep things civil. Professional despite my discomfort.

'Good morning, sir.' His responding smirk is unsettling.

'Is there anything in particular you're looking for? Perhaps there is a missus you are shopping for? Because I have this beautiful blue top that—'

'I'd like to see it on you,' he cuts in, voice raspy and blue eyes burning. 'Well, off of you, actually.'

I take a step back, feeling the grimy wall suddenly against my shoulders. My voice quivers, but I force the words out. 'I think you should leave now.'

My eyes linger on his blossoming black eye as he runs a hand through oily brown hair. His smile only grows more crazed. 'Oh, no, I'm not letting you out of my sight again, pretty.'

My lips part, allowing words to stumble out. 'Please, I—'

'Did I not take care of you properly the first time?'

That dry voice cuts through my own, full of challenge. My eyes lift to the looming figure now suddenly behind the man closing in on me.

Mak looks relaxed, bored even, as he waits expectantly with arms crossed over a broad chest. Most of his ebony hair is tied back with a strap, though several pieces fall around his face, blowing in the soft breeze. That strand of silver peeks out at me, glinting with familiarity and comfort.

Tears well at the mere sight of him.

The man whips round, eyes widening. 'Shit.'

I'm not exactly sure how it happened, seeing that I chose quite the inopportune moment to blink. But the man's face is suddenly shoved against the grimy wall beside me while the length of Mak's arm presses against the back of his neck.

'You are a pathetically slow learner,' Mak says dryly. 'I figured one black eye would be enough to get my point across. But it seems you'd like a matching one.'

'I-I didn't recognize her, I swear!' The man's voice is muffled against the brick.

Mak leans in, his voice a murmur. 'We both know why that's a lie.'

And then he's grabbing the man by the collar to roughly turn him round, shoving his back against the wall. He sputters, forcing Mak to speak over him. 'Dena, I think you should do the honors.'

'W-What?' I croak from where I'm gawking beside him.

'It will be good practice.' He says this simply, as though I have any idea of what he's suggesting. 'I would have let you punch me if it came to it, but this is a far more appealing option.'

'You . . . You want me to punch him?' I shake my head in protest. 'No, you go ahead. I'm good.'

'Dena.'

'Really, I'll leave this one up to you,' I assure with an unconvincing smile. 'This is more your thing.'

With a sigh, he reaches out a hand to close round my arm, dragging me towards him against my will. 'Come on. This is part of your training.'

He squares my shoulders, positioning me for a punch. 'Mak, I —'

'Think of what he and his friends tried to do.' His voice is a murmur. 'Think of what he will continue to try with other women in the slums.'

I take a steadying breath, letting his words sink in. But it's what he says next that has my fist flying towards the man's face.

'Think of what he would try to do to Pae.'

The man sputters, spitting blood from his mouth. Pain shoots down my arm, feeling as though my knuckles have been dipped in fire. My shout is strained. 'Plagues!'

He raises his eyebrows at my exclamation. 'Come on, tell me how you really feel.'

Hugging my hand, I glance around before quietly

proclaiming what I'd bitten back. 'Shit! That hurt like . . . like hell!'

I smile timidly despite the pain, feeling proud of my profanity. And when Mak musters the slightest smile, I know he feels the same. 'Good form, hun. Maybe you have learned something.' Then he turns to the cowering figure pinned against the wall. 'Don't let me ever see you again.'

He's gone in an instant, sprinting down the street and shoving bodies aside. Shaking out my aching hand, I watch Mak track the man's movements until he's disappeared into the crowd. 'Th-Thank you,' I whisper before letting my head fall limply against his chest.

His arms hesitate before encircling me, and I don't waste a second before doing the same. When I finally release him from my crushing hug, I clear my throat, earning his attention for my quiet question. 'What did you do that night you went looking for those men?'

He brushes stray strands of hair from his face. 'I found them.'

I lean in. 'And after that?'

He looks at me blankly. 'I thought I ensured that they would never come within your vicinity again. Clearly, I failed.'

I blink about a dozen times before finally finding my voice. 'Why did you think he was lying about not recognizing me? I mean, it was dark that one night and—'

'He was lying, Adena.' His voice cuts through my own. 'Just believe that.'

I open my mouth to spew several more questions when he suddenly steps away. 'How about a sticky bun to celebrate your first assault?'

I smack his arm lightly. 'And I don't plan on ever doing it again. My hand hurts. And I kind of need that to sew.' After a quick moment of contemplation, I add, 'But I will never turn down a sticky bun.'

His lips twitch. 'Oh, I know.'

I watch him vanish onto the street before allowing myself to slump against the wall. My heart still pounds against my chest, and I squeeze my eyes shut as if that will slow it.

A firm tap on my shoulder interrupts my deep breathing.

It's an Imperial my eyes open to, smelling of starch and frowning with indifference. I startle at the sight and stagger backwards into the wall. The man looks unfazed by this, only opening his mouth to recite the words he's been given.

'I am here to escort you to the castle.'

The stolen sticky bun flashes before my eyes, and right when I'm sure that I'll be imprisoned for my crime, he says, 'You have been summoned as a seamstress on behalf of a Purging Trials contestant.'

'Pae,' I whisper before he pushes on despite the drop of my jaw.

'Yes, for Paedyn Gray.' He looks very displeased that this is how he is spending his morning. 'She is waiting for you in the coach.'

CHAPTER 9

Adena

He looks to be guarding the sticky bun with his life. I weave between bodies, forcing my way towards him. He's wrapped his arms around my treat, protecting the precious cargo from several flying elbows.

'Mak!' My shout is swallowed up in the commotion, but I force my voice louder. 'Mak!'

When his head whips in my direction, I wave my hands in the air, jumping high enough to catch his attention. At the sight of me, I swear he smiles.

He jerks his head towards a nearby alley – a silent order to follow. I stumble behind him, pushing through

the crowd until I'm able to suck in the open air of the alleyway.

'What's going on?' He examines me closely. 'Is everything okay?'

My lips split into a smile, my voice a squeal. 'Everything is more than okay! She's here. She's here and she's taking me with her!'

'Slow down.' He steps towards me, placing a hand on my shoulder. 'Who's here?'

'Pae!' Words tumble from my mouth. 'An Imperial told me that I'm being sent to the palace to become her seamstress for the Trial's balls! Isn't that amazing? I'll get to sew her dresses and—'

'When?'

The flat tone of his voice makes me falter. 'Um, now, actually. But I told the Imperial that I had to say goodbye, so I've been trying to find you before I have to get back to him.'

'But,' his voice is alarmingly lethal, 'we have our mission tonight. We have a plan. A plan for *both* of us to sneak into the castle.'

I shake my head, hoping a smile will lighten the mood. 'Mak, your uniform is done. You are free to go to the castle whenever you—'

'No, it will be much riskier without you. I need your power there with me,' he mumbles, more to himself.

I shift on my feet. 'Look, I can see why you would be nervous to go alone. Why don't you just write Hera a note, and I can make sure it gets to—'

'You don't understand!' he shouts, shoving a hand through his disheveled hair. 'I need to be there! We were meant to go together so I could ensure you'd be in my range, but now I'll have no idea where you are . . .'

He trails off, murmuring more things I don't understand. 'Mak.' He shakes his head at the mention of his name. 'I . . . I don't understand. What are you talking about?'

I reach out a hand, hoping to run it comfortingly down his arm. But he steps back, shoving space between us. 'I need to get her out of there! Out of this kingdom! And if you're too deep within the castle, I won't be able to wield your power,' he rambles. 'Or worse, I'll run into the prince who will sense exactly what I am.'

'Wield my power?' I echo quietly.

'Yes, Adena, wield your power,' he breathes. 'Because that is what I do. What I am.' He steps towards me, forcing me back until my shoulders hit the wall. 'And now it will be even harder to save her.'

111

My mind reels, running over every bit of information given to us about the Elites. It's public knowledge that Kai Azer is the only recorded Wielder in all of Ilya. Some believe it is because no one has ever possessed such power, while others speculate that the king has ensured his son is the most powerful Elite in the kingdom by killing off any other threat.

And I think I may be staring at one. May have been staring at one for weeks.

Confusion clogs my throat, forcing me to swallow. 'You're not a Phaser.'

He laughs, the sound strained and bitter. 'No, honey. I'm not. And Hera is going to die in these Trials if I can't get her out.'

I shake my head, fighting the tears starting to sting my eyes. 'Get her *out*? You mean, run away with her?' He opens his mouth, but anger is already spitting out of mine. 'You were going to leave me! You were going to get Hera and flee the kingdom!' I suck in a quivering breath. 'You were going to die when they caught you.'

'I was bound to die anyway,' he breathes. 'It was only a matter of time before someone found out what I am. And there can only be one Wielder in the kingdom.'

My vision clouds with unshed tears. 'You lied to me. You used me.'

He shakes his head, urging me to understand. 'Hera is all I have left—'

'You had me!' I choke. 'You had me, and I would have kept your secret. You have no idea what I'm willing to do for the people I care about. But you lied.' I stumble towards the street, wiping furiously at my damp cheeks. 'At least I had the decency to say goodbye.'

I shake out of Mak's grasp, hearing the faint shout of my name as I disappear into the current of people.

CHAPTER 10

Makoto

I watch her climb into the coach, reliving the moment I watched Hera do the same.

When the door swings shut, she's sealed from sight, likely smiling with her friend as though she wasn't just wiping tears from her face. Tears that I am to blame for.

I used to wonder what it would take to break her. How long it would be before that happiness of hers was dulled like the rest of us. And now I wish I had never found out.

Because I did this to her.

I turn away when the coach begins rumbling down

the road, stealing her away from me. Loot is overflowing with gawking bystanders, all smiles and waves for their contestant who stopped by for a visit.

Pushing carelessly through the crowd, I feel the weight of every surrounding ability, each of them threatening to smother me. It's the first time in days that I've allowed myself to acknowledge the burden of it all, the sheer suffocation of power.

If only she knew what I would give to be like her, be what I lied about. Because the Wielder I am has only ever made me weak. Targeted. Alone.

But all of that was forgotten when I was with her. When I was simply a Phaser in her presence. Now I may never get the privilege of being in her presence again.

Maybe I should have let Father have his way with me. Let him finish what he started the day I earned that gash through my lips. It would have hurt less than lying to Dena through them.

But instead, I ran to Hera – and now I need to do it again. But this time, I'll be the one saving her.

I shove through the crowd, my mind on the coach that rumbles towards the castle I should be going to tonight. I'll need to rework my already risky plan, seeing that I won't have Adena's power to aid me. Sneaking around unnoticed is no longer an option. Simply posing as an Imperial is the only plan I have left.

I guess I'll find out just how convincing Adena's uniform is.

I'm suddenly standing before the door of my shop, shouldering it open with the familiar sound of screeching hinges. The room looks dull, dreary without her light to fill it. Scraps of fabric are all that remain of her, needle and thread my last tether to our time spent together.

I stride slowly around the room, surveying every surface she's left in shambles. A thin coating of honey sticks to the corner of my work table, marking her usual spot. The padded wall for her practice punches still wears the indents of her knuckles. My eyes snag on the crumbled sheets that once draped over her figure, still smelling of her skin.

I shake my head, astounded by my absurdity. This was never meant to get so out of hand. These feelings were equally unwanted and unpredictable. She was intended to be a means to an end, the first step towards a new life far away from Ilya and the threats lurking within it. I was content to use her if it meant I could smuggle Hera out of these Trials. It was the hope I held on to. Because that was all I had left.

"You had me!"

Her pained voice echoes in my skull, forcing me to relive the bitter words. But that doesn't make it true. Because I'll never be able to have her, never be able to bottle her brightness, stow away her smiles. I don't deserve her – and I've known that since the day I saw her with that godawful blue shirt.

I slump onto the edge of my bed, eyes landing on a piece of fabric littering the floor. Bending to pick it up, my thumb brushes over the jumble of loose stitches.

It's the scrap she forced me to practice on.

But it's what she's elegantly stitched up at the top that has a smile tugging at my scar.

Keep practicing!

I trace the letters over and over, reminding myself of the mission at hand. The one where I save Hera from these Trials, and myself from this kingdom.

I never imagined it would be this difficult to leave.

Because now there is her and every moment after.

I had never known happiness before her, and if there is to be an after in which she doesn't exist, I know I never will again.

Dropping the fabric, I run cool fingers over my flushed face.

I should have listened to him. Should have turned myself in like Father so desperately wanted. Because I now hold Hera's life in my hands after so many years of her doing the same for me.

I know what I have to do.

But nimble fingers and soft skin are suddenly tugging my heart in the opposite direction.

CHAPTER 11

Adena

Blood meets my tongue, leaving a particularly unpleasant tang behind.

I suck on my finger, attempting to cease the steady stream of scarlet welling on my skin. Typically, my thumb takes the most abuse from the tip of my needle, but it seems my index finger is equally in danger this evening.

I examine the mutilated skin, cursing myself for my clumsiness. My mind is far from the fabric in front of me, just as it has been since this morning. Despite my best efforts, it keeps wandering back to Loot and the boy with soot-stained hands, scarred lips, and a sliver of silver hair.

I huff, filling the empty room with my aggravation after several hours of silence. Pale moonlight streams through the dusty windows that line the walls, casting a warm glow on the colorful fabric pouring from the shelves and draping over tables.

I've spent most of my days huddled up in the sewing room, along with most of my nights. Though, I've spent as much time with Pae as her busy schedule will allow. While she trains and rests, I try my best not to bleed on the dress I'm scrambling to finish in time.

Silver, silky fabric drapes over my leg, coating me in what looks to be melted coins. Once I've ensured that nothing is leaking from my several stab wounds, I run my fingers over the material for the dozenth time. I've never felt fabric like this, let alone afforded to use it. The entirety of this vast room is stocked full of whatever supplies I could possibly dream up. Rolls of fabric litter the shelved walls while dozens of tables sit atop soft carpet, all for the seamstresses' convenience.

I think I may have died and awoken in my own, personalized heaven.

The light at my table hums with power – a fascination in itself. I'm not used to so much electricity, running water, soft mattresses. I could get accustomed to living in a castle. I could get used to truly *living*.

Taking a deep breath, I force my focus back onto the thin, draped sleeve I'm currently stitching to the gown's body. With the ball tomorrow evening, I've resigned myself to the fact that I'll be spending much of my night alone in this sewing room.

Not that I'm complaining.

With Pae fast asleep, there is not much else I'd rather be doing. Besides, I need something to take my mind off *him*.

It wasn't hard to smile and laugh with Pae after I climbed into that coach. No, it was after that was difficult. It was when she set off for dinner with the other contestants, leaving me in a sewing room of strangers, that I was finally forced to think of him. Of the betrayal that hit me like a physical blow, forcing tears to well in my eyes.

He lied to me. About his power, his plan, his *everything*.

And here I was, thinking he cared for me. Thinking that what I felt for him just might have been reciprocated.

But it's Hera he wants more than me. Hera he's willing to risk everything for.

I shake my head at the fabric I'm furiously stitching. It's treasonous to escape the Trials. How could he go through with this plan if he knows the death that awaits them when they are caught?

'I was bound to die anyway.'

His reasoning is as tragic as it is terribly true. I don't want to think about what would happen if he was discovered to be a Wielder. In short, the king would ensure that was no longer the case.

The thought has tears prickling my eyes, blurring the fabric in my lap to nothing but a silver blob. Sniffling, I pull my hair into a messy knot, blinking away the emotion.

I'm angry at him. He used me. Lied to me.

Every thought vanishes when the wall ripples beside me.

No, *someone* ripples beside me.

I jump to my feet, clutching the needle between my fingers as if it will do anything to protect me.

My eyes widen when an Imperial steps through the wall.

An Imperial with the cleanest seams I've ever seen, and black hair interrupted by a streak of silver.

His dark eyes flick over me behind the leather mask, landing on what I've pointed at his chest. 'So, this is what you meant by wielding your needle.'

That dull voice cuts through me, shocking enough to make me momentarily lose mine. 'W-What . . .' I choke on the word and attempt to try again. 'What are you doing here?'

He swallows. His discomfort is visible, evident in the shifting of his feet. It's almost as though he doesn't know what to do with himself, and if I weren't battling so many emotions at the sight of him, I might have laughed. 'I was walking the halls and felt your power.' He clears his throat at the mention of the ability he's kept hidden from me. 'I knew it was you. And I . . . I needed to see you.'

I gesture to the length of him with the needle still poised to strike. 'Is that the only reason for your visit?'

He looks away, sighing. 'Look, I came to see you first. That has to count for something.'

'Well, it doesn't.' I cross my arms, tone defiant. 'Don't let me hold you up on your way to getting yourself killed.'

'Please,' he whispers, taking a step towards me. 'Just let me explain—'

'Explain?' I laugh loud enough to have him looking around nervously. 'You had nearly two weeks to explain to me what was going on. Instead, you lied.'

I step back, my voice strained. 'And you spent every day knowing that I would never see you again after I was done making that stupid uniform for you.'

He's persistent, pushing forward as he pleads, 'Dena. Please. If you don't like what I have to say, you can stab me with your needle once I'm done.'

I eye him skeptically. 'Promise?'

He nods. 'Yes. But only because I know you wouldn't actually do it.'

I feel offended, despite knowing he's exactly right. 'You don't know that.'

'I know you,' he says softly. 'And I know that I'm the fighter, and you're the lover.'

I swallow. 'Go on.'

He takes a heavy breath, one that holds the weight of something he's carried for years. 'I ran away from home. I was fourteen at the time.' His head shakes slightly. 'Hera was only twelve, living with my family because her parents had died. She's my cousin – maybe I should have led with that.'

I struggle to hide the relief flooding to my face. He never talked about what she was to him. And I'm selfishly thankful for their relation and nothing more.

'We ran away from my parents, started living on

our own from that moment on,' he continues quietly. 'She's the only person who's been there for me. The only one who helped keep me alive while I hid in the shadows, terrified that someone would find out what I am.'

He takes a step closer, swallowing what little space remained between us. 'That is why I have to do this. I can't let her die. Not after she spent years of her life saving me.'

I'm quiet for longer than he likely expected. I watch him squirm under my scrutiny before finally saying, 'Why did you run away?'

He shakes his head slightly. 'That's a story for another time.'

'When?' I say, sounding harsher than perhaps I've ever been. 'You're here to say goodbye, aren't you? So, don't lie to me, Mak. There is no other time for me to finally get to know you.'

'There's not much worth knowing,' he murmurs.

'Fine.' I stare him down with the pointed look I learned from my mama. 'Then I think we're done here.'

'You want to get to know me?' He rips the mask from his face, revealing the strong features hidden beneath. 'I know that not a single person has convinced me to care about them before you.'

'But Hera—'

'Hera's family,' he corrects. 'But you . . . you're the embodiment of everything I am not. And yet, here I am, crawling back to you as though I've left a piece of myself behind.' He slowly lifts a hand, and I hold my breath when his fingers run down a loose curl. 'And it scares the shit out of me.'

'So,' I breathe, 'what exactly are you saying, Mak? I mean, in the simplest way possible, tell me what—'

'I regret not buying that blue shirt from you, if only so I had your attention long enough to convince you that red suits you better. I regret not telling you how much I like it when you blow those bangs out of your eyes, or the way you clap after finishing a row of stitches. I regret smothering every smile you made me want to give you. And I regret not telling you the truth. But most of all, not saying goodbye.'

My heart plummets, sinking into the stomach filled with butterflies. I can't say a thing, can't move an inch as he leans towards me and—

Footsteps echo from the hallway outside.

We jump apart, eyes flying to the closed door and

the growing sound of steps behind it. Mak fastens the mask back onto his face, his expression far too stoic for our situation.

'You need to go,' I whisper urgently. 'Imperials never come in here and if whoever that is sees you, they will know something is going on.'

'I need to get Hera,' he says evenly.

'They will catch you.' I plead with him, frantically trying to make him understand. 'For all we know that could be Kai out there.'

'Adena—'

'Go. Please,' I beg. 'There is no need for both of you to die.'

The footsteps grow louder with every second spent arguing.

He shakes his head. 'Then I have to come back tomorrow for her.'

'You can't.' My eyes are pinned on his. 'They guard the contestants' doors the night before a Trial. They would stop you before you could even make it to her.' He opens his mouth to argue, but my whisper quiets him. 'Please, Mak. Don't regret this too.'

He stares at me for a long, unblinking moment. And right when I think he's about to make a horrible decision, he strides over to one of the many windows leading to the ground outside. Before he phases through to the open air beyond, he turns to murmur, 'Come see me. Please. I don't think I can handle losing both of you.'

And then he's gone, melting through the wall and into the night.

I have just enough time to take a steadying breath before the door swings open.

My mouth drops at the sight of the man in the doorway before my knees bend into a curtsy. 'Your Highness! Um, hi – sorry – I wasn't expecting you or else I would have—'

'Not been here?' The future king laughs lightly like I've seen him do so many times with Pae.

'Maybe?' I admit with a hesitant smile.

'I don't blame you.' He shrugs. 'I'm not as much fun as I used to be.'

'Oh, I'm sure that's not true,' I laugh. And then I'm suddenly clearing my throat to ramble. 'I mean, not that I think you're lying, of course. It's just that I know Pae enjoys her time with you so . . . You can't be too boring?' I end the sentence with an unsure question while fighting the urge to flee the room.

I should really work on keeping my mouth shut.

'Does she now?' he asks, sounding amused. 'That is news to me. I was beginning to think she despised me.'

'Well, she should know better than to despise you.' I sigh, shaking my head. 'Your Highness,' I add quickly. 'But she doesn't always do what she knows she should.'

He nods in agreement, a slight smile on his face. 'That, I have learned.' He strides over to the illuminated table draped in silver fabric. 'That is actually why I was hoping to find you here.'

'R–Really?' I stutter, my smile widening. 'What could you possibly need from me?'

'For starters,' he sighs, 'I need you to start calling me Kitt, not "Your Highness". Then, I need some advice.'

I beam. 'I think I can do both of those things for you, Kitt.'

'Perfect.' He clasps his hands in front of his navy tunic. 'Now, is this the dress she'll be wearing to the first ball?'

I nod vigorously. 'Isn't it beautiful? Ugh, I can't wait to see it on her. And the cut of it will really accentuate her—' I press my lips together at the reminder of who I'm talking to. 'You get the point. It will look great.'

'Oh, I'm sure it will.' He sighs, looking unsure. 'She will definitely be making a statement.'

I fight to hide my frown. 'And you don't want her to?'

'I want her to be careful, that's all.' He runs his fingers over the smooth fabric. 'There are people out there who will take offense at her boldness. You know, not wearing green as is tradition.'

I nod slowly, unsure of what to say. Thankfully, he speaks instead. 'So, what do you think? Tux and a black tie?' He runs a hand through messy, blond hair. 'Not that it matters. I doubt very many people will be looking at me anyway.'

I giggle softly in agreement. 'Wear a silver tie clip. And don't be offended if she doesn't even notice. But it will be a nice touch for those who care enough to look closely.'

'Oh, there is always someone looking closely,' he breathes before falling silent.

The light hums atop the table; the only sound for several seconds. That's before I clear my throat to say, 'Well, I'm always available for all your fashion needs!'

His eyes meet mine. 'Can you tell me what I'm doing wrong?'

The question startles me for a moment. 'With your outfit?' I look him over. 'I mean, that color definitely complements your skin tone—'

'No,' he chuckles. 'Paedyn. She will hardly look at me.' He lifts his hands in exasperation, scoffing slightly. 'I mean, I'm not sure what to do anymore. I find her fascinating in a way that no one has ever been before. Like she's realer than anything I've encountered here in the castle.'

I smile at the sound of his voice, at the sincerity coating each word. I can sense a smittenness I doubt he's even acknowledged yet. And part of me hopes to see my best friend beside him with a genuine smile on her face.

Maybe in another life they were meant to be. A life where he wasn't the heir to an Elite throne, and Pae wasn't punished for being an Ordinary.

'Pae is a difficult creature.' I place a hand on my hip. 'Trust me, I know this firsthand. But she's consistent with what she wants the most from others.' I shrug. 'Honesty. Someone she can talk to. And for you especially, an open mind to what she has to say.'

He nods absentmindedly. 'An open mind, huh?'

I nod. 'You're the future king. I can imagine she has a lot of suggestions for you.'

He chuckles. 'I'm sure she does.' Then he's turning towards the door. 'Thank you, Adena. But you may not be rid of me yet. I'll likely need more advice in the future.'

My grin is wide. 'And I'll be here for as long as you'll allow!'

He returns my smile. 'Once I'm king, I may just need to make you an adviser of mine.'

CHAPTER 12

Makoto

I've been hammering steel since I saw her.

I don't think I've stopped for longer than it took to choke down some food. Channeling every emotion into a physical blow is the only thing keeping me sane these past twenty-four hours.

Because I failed Hera. Damned her to death. And the guilt of that is threatening to swallow me whole.

I should have gone to her first, should never have been so distracted by Adena. But the pull of her power was so familiar, so comforting, that I couldn't help but follow the feel of it. The presence of her is hypnotizing. So much so that I missed my chance to save Hera.

Guilt has my hammer slamming into the steel, over and over. The rhythmic sound lulls me into a state of detachment, numbing any notion of feeling.

The metal glows red.

I couldn't save her.

My hammer hits hard.

She will die in these Trials.

A wave of heat hits my face.

I failed—

Hair stands on the back of my neck at the familiar feel of her.

I straighten, dropping my tools to the ground as the power grows with each passing second. My eyes drift to the door, feeling each step she takes towards it.

When she knocks, I almost laugh.

Whipping open the door, I'm met with wide eyes and a timid smile. She gives me about three seconds to stare before her arms are around me, squeezing tighter than I imagined she'd be able.

After a moment, my hands find her back, holding her tightly against my chest. 'You're here.'

Her voice is muffled. 'Only because you are.'

I smile at her words. 'You know you can just walk through the door, right?'

'I didn't want to scare you.'

'I can sense you, hun.' I breathe in the sweet scent of her hair. 'I always know when you're near.'

'Right.' I feel her shrug. 'I'm still getting used to that.'

'And I'm still getting used to you knowing that.'

She pulls away, looking up at me with those big eyes. 'But there is still a lot more I need to know.'

'Oh, is that right?'

'It is.' She grins mischievously. 'And you still owe me a night in the Fort, remember?'

'I don't recall ever having an urge to do that.'

She huffs, fitting her hand into mine before dragging me out of the door. 'We had a deal, Mak!'

'A deal implies that this is mutually beneficial.'

'Oh, you're so dramatic,' she teases unsympathetically.

We weave down the dark streets, hand in hand. She's nestled close to my side, seemingly blissfully unaware of her surroundings when she's in my presence. I guide us through the shadows, allowing her the luxury of looking anywhere but in front of her.

After I've steered her by the shoulders for the second time, she looks up suddenly to say, 'Thank you. For leaving last night.'

I nod slightly at the reminder of what I didn't do.

Noticing this, she adds, 'Are you all right?'

I consider this for a long moment. 'I never really was.'

'I'm sorry you couldn't save her,' she whispers. 'But you did everything you could.'

'Not everything.'

She frowns up at me. 'The ball is happening as we speak, and after that, Hera will be guarded until the Trial. Getting caught wasn't going to help anyone.'

I shrug. 'It would certainly speed up the inevitable.'

'You won't get caught,' she huffs. 'There are very few people who know what you are and, lucky for you, I'm fabulous at keeping secrets.'

Tapping a finger against her full lips, she adds, 'And what makes you so sure Hera can't survive these Trials? She's a Veil, after all.' Adena offers me a sympathetic smile. 'She might not need to be saved.'

I nod numbly, remembering all the years Hera has survived in the slums. Maybe I have underestimated her. And maybe that is exactly what she will tell me on the other side of these Trials.

'I hope you're right,' I manage gruffly.

Silence stretches between us until she can no longer handle the absence of conversation. 'This is probably not the time to ask — actually, it definitely isn't — but how did the Imperial uniform do? Any suspicion from the other guards?'

I shake my head. 'They barely even glanced at me. After walking for nearly an hour and a half to get to the castle, I continued right through the entrance closest to the Bowl. As if I had just come in from a rotation.'

I can see the smile she's attempting to hide. 'Well, I'm glad my work was convincing.'

'Yeah, it was perfect.' I sigh. 'And all for nothing. I'm sorry I wasted your time.'

'I was with you.' She smiles softly. 'How could that have been a waste of time?'

I don't have a chance to answer before she pulls me round a corner, leading us towards a dead end. 'Here we are!' she exclaims far too enthusiastically at the sight of a dark alley. 'Home sweet home!'

Stepping closer, I catch sight of a miscellaneous mound of items, all piled together to create a barrier against the wall. It's nearly three feet tall and sitting atop several rugs and ragged blankets. 'This,' I say slowly, 'is where you sleep?'

'Yep! This is Pae's side.' She gestures to the left side of a worn rug. 'Which obviously makes this half my side.' After phasing through the barrier of trash, she then plops down onto her designated area of the rug. 'This spot is reserved for Pae, but I'll make an exception tonight.'

'Oh, lucky me,' I mutter, slowly beginning to muster the strength to sit down on the filthy rug. 'Plagues, this place is a shithole.'

'Hey!' The back of her hand meets my stomach. 'It's home.'

'Well, your home is a shithole.'

She gives me a pointed look. 'You don't have to be rude.'

'Have you met me?' I ask this very genuinely.

'I have. And I think you're kinder than you let on.' If her answer wasn't equally as genuine, I might have laughed.

'And what makes you think that?'

She looks suddenly timid, slightly unsure. 'You're the only one who wanted to buy my blue shirt.'

My confession comes racing back to me, as though it was much longer than a handful of hours ago that I spewed it. I had been so focused on Hera's fate that the hushed spilling of my heart has yet to cross my mind. But now that it has, I'm flustered at the sight of her. At the reminder of every word I uttered.

'Do you still want to?' she asks quietly.

I nod slowly, my eyes never leaving hers. 'Only if you will let me tell you something in exchange for my business.'

'Deal,' she breathes, fighting a smile.

Reaching into my pocket, I pull out a single shilling to offer her. She stares at it. 'I was selling it for three.'

'Yeah,' I draw out the word, 'and how was that working out for you?'

She crosses her arms. 'Three.'

'I didn't realize you were in any position to negotiate.'

'Two,' she amends. 'And a smile.'

I visibly weigh the offer, tilting my head back and forth. 'That's a bit steep, honey.'

She sighs. 'Just the smile, then.'

'That was the steep part I was referring to.'

Her words are gentle, as though she's speaking to a spooked animal. And, in a way, that's a fair comparison. 'Will you tell me? About you? About why you won't smile for me?'

'It's not personal, Dena.' I shift to lean against the wall, draping my arms over bent knees. 'It's just something I stopped doing the day Hera and I ran away from home.'

She raises her eyebrows in silent encouragement to

continue, to which I blow out a breath of annoyance. 'Fine, but I'm getting that damn shirt for free, then.' I take a pause, collecting my thoughts before continuing, 'I grew up on the other side of the slums. My parents were – well, are – the very definition of poor Mundanes. They could barely feed themselves, let alone any children. Long story short and private details later, they unexpectedly had me.

'It wasn't much of a childhood, really.' I say this with a shrug, as if it had little impact on who I turned into. 'They didn't want to have a kid and never intended on feeding another mouth. But there I was, begrudgingly forcing them into parenthood.'

She listens intently, head tilted, eyes wide, elbows on her knees and face in her palms. It's endearing at least. Adorable at most.

'Like all Elite toddlers, I couldn't control my abilities, but seeing that my mother was a Sight and my father a Bluff, they figured I was simply another Mundane to litter the slums.' I sigh. 'Well, until I got old enough to draw on the more physical powers of those in my vicinity.

'I almost lit our shack of a home on fire when I was five. This led my parents to believe that I was a late bloomer, but a Burner, nonetheless. That is, until I began crawling up the walls within the same hour.'

I glance over at her, finding a dramatic look of awe on her face. If it were anyone else, I might have thought they were mocking me. But it's Adena, and this look is mild compared to the one she gives me at the sight of sticky buns.

'What then?' she urges, waving a hand encouragingly.

'Then they started to figure out what I was.' My voice is dull, masking the bitterness biting each word. 'They didn't know what to do with me. Kept me locked inside our little shack. Hera was the first person I remember seeing other than my parents. She showed up on our doorstep when I was seven, and we quickly became inseparable, seeing that we had no one else.'

I hadn't noticed my thumb was trailing the length of that scar cutting my lips until I catch her gaze tracing the movement. 'As I got older, I began to understand why it was that I wasn't allowed out. I was still learning to control my abilities, and being a Wielder means certain death. I was – I am – a threat to the king because of a power I didn't ask for. My parents knew this, and it was clear that I was unwanted. Especially by my father.'

I glance up at Adena, hoping for a reason to end this conversation, though I find nothing but concern in her hazel gaze. Nothing but gentleness guiding her hand towards my knee, seeping comfort from every splayed finger.

'He thought I was useless — told me as much.' Swallowing, I attempt not to stumble through each word in my haste to get them out of my mouth. 'I couldn't work at the shop with him, couldn't leave the house without fear of being found out. I was an expense. A nuisance. A disappointment.'

'You're not,' Adena breathes, shaking her head firmly.

'Oh, I was.' I nod, my eyes drifting up to the sky above us. 'I just wasn't fortunate enough to be loved despite it.'

When my eyes find hers, I regret having said anything at all. It's as though every word has dulled the sparkle in her eyes, smothered her smile into a dreariness undeserving of her lips. I never imagined she could look so grim. And I hate that I'm the cause of it.

But knowing she won't allow me to stop now, I continue with a deep breath. 'I had Hera. My parents tolerated her more than they did me, seeing that she earned money by performing street magic as a Veil, but things only grew worse as we got older. Father started drinking more heavily, and Mother did nothing to stop it. And that is when I began learning how to defend myself.'

I run a hand through my hair, shaking my head at the flood of memories beginning to surface. 'He would come home late from the shop, occasionally bringing back the weapons he'd made that day. He would yell; Mother would hide. I took the brunt of it, shielded both Hera and my mother when it came to it. It was me he was angry with. Me who was useless to him.'

A hand is now covering her mouth, hiding a half of her shocked face. 'Is that why you ran away?'

'Yes and no. I was fourteen when my shitty life officially fell apart.' She scoots towards me, her hand still sympathetically squeezing my knee. 'The night it happened was the same as usual. Father came home drunk, ready to pick a fight. He'd walked in on Hera and me laughing about something one of us had said. That's when I saw the flash of a sword in his hand. I'd seen him with weapons before, but nothing so sharp, so lethal.

'I tucked Hera behind me, as I usually did, and looked around for a mother who was never there. But it wasn't the sword that scared me the most, but Father's words.' I swallow. 'I'll never forget what he said to me that night. He said I would be more use to him if they'd just handed me over to the king. If they had sold me out instead of putting up with me for so many years. And then . . .' I blink, feeling emotion beginning to build there. Hating it, I push on, my voice stern. 'And then he threatened to do just that. Said he'd sell me to the king for the shillings he deserved, and that he should have done it years ago.'

'Mak . . .' Adena's voice is barely a whisper, barely audible over my shaky breaths.

'I didn't deserve to smile. That is what he told me.' My voice grows quieter with each word slipping from my past and haunting my present. 'I don't remember the sword swinging towards me, only his voice when he promised to wipe that smile from my face.'

My thumb finds the scar cutting my lips and shakily traces it. 'It was after he cut me that Hera and I ran. I . . . I didn't know what he would do to her, and I couldn't wait around to see if he would make good on his promise to sell me to the king.'

I can't look at her, not after what I've said. 'Hera and I survived in the slums for several years before we were able to afford a real roof over our heads.' Still avoiding her sorrowful stare, I add, 'I forced myself to control the overwhelming power. Learned to hide in plain sight. And then I become a blacksmith, just to spite my father. So, something good came out of it.'

My eyes squeeze shut when her fingers graze my chin.

She turns my face towards her despite my resistance. Her palm is soft against my cheek, foreign in its comfort. But when her thumb brushes my scar, I finally meet her gaze.

'He stole your smile,' she whispers, tears clinging to dark lashes. 'No wonder you didn't have one to give me.'

Regret rams into me once again, her words a reminder of every missed opportunity to make her smile with one of my own. 'I'll find one,' I murmur. 'Steal it back if I must. For you.'

Her lips lift, eyes shining with tears. 'And I'll cherish it.'

Her thumb is warm against my skin as it continues to trace the scar, creating new memories to associate with it. After a long stretch of silence, she allows herself a quiet question. 'Where are they now? Your parents?'

I shrug slightly as though I don't think of it daily. 'I'm not sure. Probably in that same house on the opposite side of the slums. But I've hidden from them for years, masking myself in the masses. And I'm not dead yet, so I figured Father never made it to the king.' I scoff. 'They must be satisfied enough with my absence.'

She nods slowly, taking in my words before making a proclamation of her own. 'You are far from useless. You are strong and clever and can really pull off an Imperial uniform. In the best way possible.' Her eyes are full of fire even with her thumb still pressed against my lips. 'And no one can take away your smile. It's yours to give, Mak.'

I grab her wrist, gently pulling it down enough for me to speak. 'Makoto.'

Her lashes flutter. 'W-What?'

'Makoto,' I mutter. She squeaks when I tug her towards me with the wrist I'm still holding and a hand behind her knee. 'My name is Makoto Khitan.' Her eyes widen, closer to mine then they ever have been. 'Now you can properly scold me.'

I hear her swallow. 'And what else should I know about you, Makoto?'

Tilting my head in a sort of shrug, I say, 'This may come as a shock to you, but I can be a bit . . . blunt at times.'

She smiles encouragingly. 'Self-awareness is the first step to change.'

'Oh, I'm not planning on changing. I was just ensuring that you knew this was a recurring thing. Now, what else?' I sigh. 'I've never been able to skip properly, not sure why that is or why I'm embarrassed about that fact. Oh, I'm not a fan of spoons, only forks. I enjoy radishes more than the average person. And I've never been much good with a bow.'

I watch her reactions to my words – how they start in her eyes before spreading to the rest of her face. 'Go on. I know there's more.'

'Sorry, hun. Your turn.' My eyes flick between hers. 'I'm going to need some details in return.'

She smiles, effortlessly dazzling. 'Oh, well, that might take a while.'

'You really think I was going to get any sleep down here?' I raise my eyebrows. 'No, I have every intention of talking about you till morning.'

And then I take a slow breath, allowing myself something that I haven't had any desire to do before meeting her.

And, terrifyingly, it comes easily.

I smile.

CHAPTER 13

Adena

'Pae is not going to be happy about you scrubbing the tub.'

I singsong my warning, smiling at her crouched form as I say it.

With brown hair tied up in a knot, Ellie whips her head towards me, sending wispy strands blowing into her eyes. 'Then she never need know about it.'

I cross my arms, looking down my nose at her teasingly. 'And you trust me enough not to tell her?'

Ellie lifts her sponge, dripping water as she points the dull end at me. She smiles softly. 'If I go down, you go down with me. Besides, I'm her maid. This is what I do.'

I sigh, leaning against the door frame of the bathroom. The entirety of Paedyn's room is spotless, seeing that she's been gone for nearly a full week now in the first Trial. All of it is very unnerving, and I don't like the idea of Pae being in these *special* Trials. It's hard enough to survive as it is.

At that gloomy thought, I turn my attention back to Ellie now loudly scrubbing the bottom of the tub. 'Any ideas for her next gown? The second ball is already in a week.'

'Not really.' She's forced to raise her voice over the water that is now running. 'Who knows what color she will be wanting next?'

'Well, I'll just have to wait for her to tell me, then.' I say this confidently, as though I know for a fact that she will be coming back alive today. 'Because the silver dress will be difficult to top. Ugh, she looked so stunning with the drooping sleeves and slitted skirt—'

'And you didn't even get to see her turning heads at the ball.' Ellie peeks up at me, pressing her lips together in a knowing smile.

'Well,' I say, flustered, 'I was there to help her get ready and wish her luck, of course . . .'

'Right.' Ellie's smile is far too mischievous for her

sweet features. 'Because you were busy seeing your *boy*.'

'He's not . . . He's not my *boy*, Ellie,' I scold despite the smile beginning to form on my lips. 'And I don't regret sneaking out one bit. I took him to the Fort, and we talked for hours about every little detail.' I can feel my cheeks heating at the thought. 'He told me that he had a dog growing up. Well, it was a stray that would come and visit him, but isn't that adorable? I learned all about his favorite things and how he prefers green apples to red— Oh! And he said my hair is – and I quote – very bouncy.'

I beam, forcing myself to take a breath. 'Anyways, I've seen him almost every day since. Sometimes we meet halfway, or I leave early in the evening so I get to the slums before dark. No one seems to care where I go, so long as I'm back in time to make Pae's dress.'

Ellie lets me finish my squeal before saying, 'Wow, you really are falling for him.'

I still my dancing feet at her words. Falling is not what I do. No, I trip into love, unable to slow down long enough to question these feelings or the person I've dumped them on. But I've liked boys in the past, and nothing compares to how easily I'm tripping into this one.

'Have you told Paedyn?'

I blink out of my daze. 'Hmm?'

Ellie narrows her eyes slightly. 'You haven't told her, have you?'

I huff, plopping down on the spotless floor beside her, one I'm suspecting she scrubbed before I arrived. 'No, I haven't. But I will! Just not . . . yet.' I pick at my fingers, falling into the same dilemma I've had since being reunited with Paedyn. 'She has so much on her plate at the moment, and she needs to keep her focus on the Trials. I don't want my love life to be a distraction for her. Because, trust me, Pae would not stop until she met Mak and approved.' I shake my head, making up my mind. 'No, I can't have her losing her focus or worrying about anything to do with me when her own life is at stake.'

Ellie's silent for a long moment before nodding slowly. 'She won't be happy about being left in the dark.'

I smile, small and teasing as I nod towards the bathtub. 'Same goes for your cleaning, my dear Ellie.'

Before she can splash me with water, I hurry from the room, shouting, 'I'll be back! I'm off to meet my boy!'

It's an effort not to skip down the hallway in excitement. I can hardly contain my anticipation to—

I nearly run into a large figure rounding the corner.

In the midst of my sputtered apology, my eyes trail up to the green ones boring down at me. I blink, horrified by what I've just done, and sweep into a curtsy.

'Your Majesty!' I squeak. 'I am so very sorry! I really must get better at watching where I'm going, especially in such a crowded castle where—'

A large, raised hand has the remaining words dying in my throat. My eyes flick from the palm hovering before my face to the man standing behind it.

Everything about the king is large and looming. He stands well over a foot above me, and his piercing gaze feels as though it might cleave me in half. Swallowing, I stand before him as his scrutiny sweeps over me, lingering on my messy hair and crumpled clothing.

When his silencing hand finally falls, I feel oddly stripped bare before him. 'And who might you be?'

His voice is deep in a way that is far from comforting. I shift on my feet, attempting to sound at ease as I say, 'I'm Adena, Your Majesty. What a pleasure it is to meet you!'

The smile he gives me is menacing at best. 'Let's not lie to your king, Adena. I'm likely the last person you wish to see, seeing that you're in such a hurry to find someone else.'

My mouth opens and closes several times before words begin to fall out. 'Oh, well, I just have a lot of work to do before the next ball and was hoping to get a head start on things. You know, picking fabric and calculating measurements—'

His hand lifts once again.

'I haven't seen you before,' he says evenly. 'Why are you here?'

'Oh, I'm Paedyn's seamstress.' I say this as cheerily as I can muster. 'She sent for me since I've gotten quite good at making clothes for her over the years.'

He contemplates this with narrowed eyes. 'You are close with Paedyn, I take it?'

'Yes, very.' I smile, relieved to be talking about something so comforting. 'We've lived in the slums together for years. So, it's no shock that we are the best of friends!'

'I see,' he hums. 'She must be very happy to have you here with her.'

I nod. 'Oh, yes, we both are!'

'Well, you will be happy to know that she survived this first Trial.' His tone is dull, as if he'd been hoping for a very different outcome.

I suppress my relieved sigh. 'Of course she did!

I'd expect nothing less from Pae.'

'*Pae*,' he repeats softly, lifting the edge of his mouth in that unnerving way. 'How sweet.'

I do my best to keep the smile on my face, even as I'm shifting uncomfortably on my feet. I'm about to attempt a quick curtsy and swift escape when he sighs. 'Yes, how fortunate that Pae was not one of the casualties this Trial.'

I blink. 'Um, if you don't mind me asking – Your Majesty – who were the casualties?'

He shrugs slightly, as though these deaths mean little to him. 'Sadie – a shame. I'm close with her father. Oh, and the Veil girl from the slums, though that was unsurprising . . .'

His voice fades, muffling as my ears begin to ring. My eyes fix on the wall behind him, glazing over as the gravity of his words weigh down on me.

Hera is dead.

All I can think of is Mak. Of the guilt on his face when he finds out, the agony in his voice following every word after.

'How terrible,' I say shakily. 'I'm so sorry to hear that.'

His voice is eerily cheery. 'Such is the Trials.'

When he says nothing else, I sink into a wobbly curtsy. 'It was an honor meeting you, Your Majesty.'

I move to scurry past him and startle when his booming voice follows me down the hall. 'Oh, I'm sure we will be meeting again, Adena.'

★

Late afternoon light paints Loot in a warm glow by the time I step onto the busy street.

I would have run the whole way here if it weren't for my lack of endurance proving that to be difficult. But I followed the path down by the Bowl Arena with much more haste than usual.

The street is packed with shouting customers and squealing children. I push my way through as politely as possible, eyes trained on the crumbling building that houses his shop and home.

I'm not sure how I made it to his looming door, but I'm suddenly standing before it. I raise a hand to knock and—

And the door swings open.

I still at the sight of him.

He's standing there, eyes glossy and brimming with a guilt that tells me he already knows why I'm here.

'I felt you coming,' he whispers, voice weak.

My eyes drift to the crumpled paper clutched in his hand, catching the familiar lettering scrawled across it.

A flyer for the Trials.

What a horrible way to find out.

Tears well in my eyes as I take a step towards him. 'Oh, Mak . . .'

His composure crumples before his body suddenly crashes into mine.

He slumps against me, shoulders shaking as I wrap my arms tightly round him. The flyer showcasing Hera's death flutters to the ground, forgotten in the wave of emotions threatening to drown him. His body shudders against mine, limbs limply draped round me.

'She's gone,' he chokes out. 'She's gone, and it's all my fault.'

Sniffling, I whisper, 'No, it's not. Don't you go thinking this is your fault.'

Sobs rack his body, shaking the two of us where we stand in the doorway. 'It should have been me.' His arms clutch my waist, holding onto me for support. 'It should have been me.'

'Shh.' I run a hand down the back of his hair, feeling hot tears slip from my eyes. 'It's gonna be okay.'

'Dena.' His voice is a whisper, a guilty confession. 'It

159

should have been me. I wish it was me.'

'Don't say that.' I squeeze him tighter, feeling his body shake with each breath. 'I need you.'

'Don't,' he murmurs against my hair. 'I'll only disappoint you.'

CHAPTER 14

Adena

Over the next several days, it is a personal goal of mine to see Mak smile.

This task is most definitely not for the faint of heart. But it's rewarding in a way that keeps me searching for any sign of even the slightest smile.

And that is what has led us to tonight's activity.

'This is bullshit.'

And someone is not very enthusiastic about it.

'Wow, you were not kidding.' I smother my laugh with a hand before forcing enough composure to continue. 'You really can't skip.'

'I'm done,' he huffs, heading for his door to abandon

the alley we are practicing in. 'I've lived this long without being able to do it.'

'Come on!' I chase after him, grabbing an arm to slow him. 'Just a little more practice and you'll have it. This will take your mind off things.'

He spins, his face accusing. 'Did you need to practice?'

'Well . . . No, but—'

'See, you're a natural at this happy, girly shit.' He shakes his head. 'I – as shocking as it may seem – am not.'

'Right,' I lower my voice, forcing it to sound gruff, 'you're all brooding and rough with your sharp knives and lack of smiles.'

He crosses his arms over his chest. 'Oh, is that what I'm like?'

'And what you sound like.' I smile. 'Sort of.'

'Fine.' He gives me that sarcastic smile, though his eyes are still clouded with the sorrow of losing Hera. 'Well, you are all giggles and perpetual happiness with your bows and other frilly . . . things.'

I nod slowly, stepping towards him. 'And do you like that about me?'

He doesn't need a moment to ponder. 'Among several other things.'

'Good,' I say simply, placing a hand on my hip. 'Because I'm not changing. I like my frilly, girly things.'

'Oh, I know.'

'See, I'm a—'

'Lover not a fighter,' he finishes for me.

I beam. 'Exactly. Which is why punching that guy in the face a while ago was the absolute last thing I wished to be doing.'

Mak shrugs. 'He deserved it. And you needed the practice.'

That moment comes rushing back to me after being buried by the shock of everything that came after. The man's black eye and visible fear at the sight of Mak. The pain shooting down my arm when my fist connected with his face – a feeling I never wish to experience again.

But when I'm suddenly reminded of Mak's words to the man, my curiosity has me asking once again, 'Speaking of that day, how did you know that man was lying when he said he didn't recognize me?'

'Dena, we've been over this,' he exhales. 'I just know.'

'How?' I urge.

'This is ridiculous.'

'Don't make me scold you, Makoto Khitan,' I warn with a wag of my finger.

'Fine.' He closes the distance between us easily. 'I know because I ensured he would never forget what you looked like. Ensured that he would know exactly who you are and never take a step towards you.' He takes a breath, his face close. 'Except that he did. And I failed.'

I shake my head, mouth hanging ridiculously open. 'W–What? What do you mean you ensured he would never forget what I looked like?'

He's silent for a long moment before murmuring a string of words that have me further gawking. 'I made him, and every other man I found, memorize every one of your features. I described the color of your eyes and the length of the lashes lining them. The warmth of your skin, and the specific curl of your hair. Your nose, your lips, your smile. Down to the very scar on your palm from one of my daggers, I made them memorize you. So, yes, he knew exactly who you were and still decided to ignore my threats.'

Silence stretches between us as I stare up at him.

His expression warms at the sight of mine, though I don't miss the sadness behind his gaze. Even in the midst of mourning, he manages to muster the beginning of a smile. 'I didn't know it was possible to render you speechless.'

'I just . . .' I shake my head, trying to find the words. 'I just can't believe you would do all that for me.' He smiles slightly as I continue, 'And yet, you refuse to learn how to skip.'

With that, he's pushing me away with a palm to the forehead. I beam, happy to be his distraction. His bright spot within the bleak.

'I would argue that nothing I could do for you would top this humiliation,' he says dryly.

My giggle follows him to the end of the alley.

And I clap when he resumes his attempted skipping.

CHAPTER 15

Makoto

'What did I say about sleeping in this shithole?'

She smiles, folding her long legs beneath her, looking impossibly comfortable atop the scratchy rugs behind the Fort. 'Um, that you loved it and would be happy to stay again if it meant spending more time with me?'

I roll my eyes. 'Those words certainly didn't come out of my mouth, but I can't argue with that last part.'

She flashes one of those smiles at me, the type that makes it hard to look away. 'Good. Because I decided that we should visit the Fort on the night of each ball.'

She tears off a piece of sweet dough from the sticky bun I surprised her with. 'Call it superstition, but we were here the night of the first ball, and Paedyn is still alive and well. So I plan on continuing our tradition.'

Hera isn't.

Ignoring that thought, just as I have been every day, I say slowly, 'Well, a visit implies that I won't have to sleep here, so . . .'

'Oh, yes you will!' she huffs. 'It wasn't that bad last time.'

'My back is still sore.'

'It's been a week!'

I falter at the realization.

It's been a week.

A week since I tore that flyer from a crumbling wall, skimming it over to find that Hera was stabbed to death in the first Trial.

A week since I wept in Adena's arms. Felt her soothing touches. Voiced my guilt, my regret, my fears.

A week since I began mourning the loss of her.

But I've cried enough, drowned the pain in my tears. It all feels dull now, though the memory of her is anything but. I'm tired of the tears, the constant state of despair. Hera would scold me for hurting so much at the loss of her. She would quietly tell me to pull myself together, just as she had so many times over the years.

So, here I am, attempting to do just that. Though I've had quite the distraction to keep me company.

'Fine,' I say, accepting Adena's offer. 'The Fort it is. Thank the Plague I only have to do this one more time after tonight.'

'Great!' She squeals slightly, giddy at my agreement. 'And before I know it, Pae will be back to keep me company.'

Before I can offer my sarcasm, she's speaking again. 'Oh, that reminds me! We need to redecorate before she gets home!'

She frowns at the blank look on my face. I gesture around us. 'Sure, knock yourself out, honey.'

'Makoto,' she says sternly. The sound of my full name falling from her lips has my own quirking. 'It will only take a minute. Come on, up you go.'

After begrudgingly climbing to my feet, I discover that it would not, in fact, take a minute. Adena has me securing yarn on either side of the alley walls, stretching it over the length of the Fort. She then proceeds to stitch squares of fabric across it, creating a colorful banner she likes to call 'festive but not seeming too shocked that she survived'.

It wasn't long before I was being forced to rearrange the assortment of garbage they sleep behind, organizing the barrier in a 'more appealing manner', or so she believes. With finishing touches that include a seemingly new blanket and a single pillow to share, I'm finally allowed to take a seat.

'See!' Adena claps her hands from where she admires the slightly less shitty sleeping arrangement. 'So much better. Pae will be so shocked.'

I bite into the sticky bun, my tone mocking as I mutter, 'Yes, nothing says "welcome home" like a newly arranged pile of garbage.'

She puts a hand on her hip. 'This pile of garbage is all I've got.'

'I thought you had me?'

Her eyes flutter in a way that makes me wonder how to get her to do it again. 'Do I?'

I swallow, forcing the feeble words from my mouth. 'So long as you'll take me.'

'And if I don't?' she asks softly.

'Then no one ever will.'

Her eyes wander over me, and I can't say I dislike the

feel of it. After clearing her throat and looking away timidly, she walks towards the barrier before phasing right through it.

Our shoulders brush when she sits beside me, and I tense at the feel of it. Not because I don't want her, but because I'm so unused to someone wanting me. Choosing me. Finding me worth the effort.

Because I'm completely undeserving of it. Of her. If darkness is the absence of light, then that is what I am when she is not around. And I wonder how I've stumbled this long without her to guide me.

'What is it like?' Her question unexpectedly forces me from my thoughts. 'Having all that power?'

I don't even hesitate. 'Lonely.'

'Because no one knows about you?'

I nod. 'And I know about everyone else.'

'Everyone is told that Kai is the most powerful Elite in decades,' she says softly. 'And yet, here you are, sharing his power and living in the slums.'

'Hiding in the slums,' I spit bitterly.

She sighs, sounding shockingly frustrated. 'Do you really think the king would kill you if he knew you were a Wielder?'

'I think he would see me as nothing but a threat to

him,' I say dully. 'Just like the Fatals. He only kept one of each and now has a Wielder who happens to be a son he can control.'

She studies me as though I'm one of her rows of stitches. 'You two seem oddly similar. In more ways than just ability.'

'Well, he's done a lot of shit. And I'm just pretty shitty.' I take another bite of honey-drenched dough. 'I'm sure we'd be the best of friends under different circumstances.'

Her responding hum tells me she agrees. And, apparently, that is the only answer she cares to offer. She's suddenly very distracted by the trail of curls falling across her shoulders, and, now, so am I. What did I say to her about them? Ah, yes. Something profoundly akin to them being *bouncy*.

What a pathetic attempt at nonchalance. As if I don't admire the shine of each ringlet, or the way they cling to one another in an intertwining hug. As if I can't stop myself from staring at the column of her neck when she pulls that curly hair into a messy knot, the forgotten strands like swirling ink down her back.

As if I can stop myself from admiring how easily a laugh parts her soft lips. The way the sun warms her skin, as though she was meant to be cloaked in light. It's how joy bubbles out of her in the form of clapping hands and endearing rambles. It's the way my thoughts never cease to wander towards her, my heart falling senselessly after.

And I fear that I've admired every inch of her.

'I have something for you.'

She follows this admission with a soft giggle that is equally uneasy and intoxicating. Leaning back on my forearms, I voice my wishful thinking. 'I do hope it's a bed.'

'Nope,' she answers far too cheerily. 'Even better. I hope.'

'Little else is more appealing than sleeping through the night.' I look up at her fidgeting form, crossed legs bouncing rhythmically. 'But give it your best shot, hun.'

A look of immense distress contorts her face. 'Well, now I'm nervous!' She lifts a hand. 'That's it. I can't give it to you now. It's not ready.'

'Plagues, what have I done?' I mutter. 'Come on, Dena. Let me see it. I'm sure it's . . . fabulous – or whatever other fluffy word you like to use.'

Her eyes flutter shut when she takes a deep breath. So ridiculously dramatic, this one. 'Okay, okay.' It's with a sudden determination that her eyes open. 'I've been working on something during my free time at the castle. And I noticed that you don't have anything to carry your knives in. Soooo,' she draws out the word, 'I figured I'm pretty qualified to help you with that – I mean, I made Pae's vest, after all, and that has played a pivotal part in her thieving career—'

'The sheer number of words you speak each day is astounding—'

'—because the design is unique to her needs,' she finishes, unfazed by my interruption. 'So, I did the same for you.'

After I've nodded my encouragement several times, she finally slips something from the cloth bag beside her. She displays the item with outstretched arms as I run my gaze over the thick fabric paired with the same white leather used to make my Imperial mask.

I blink, bewildered by the beautiful weapons belt before me, equipped with uniquely sized holsters for each of my knives. Reaching out, I trace the patches of leather with my fingers, feeling each careful stitch and stretch of durable fabric.

I feel her eyes on me as I sit up slowly, taking the gift gently from her hands. 'Do you . . .' She trails off before starting again with a small smile. 'Do you like it? I can extend the pockets for each knife, if you like. I wasn't really sure how long to make them . . .'

'No.' My voice is quietly firm. 'No, I want it exactly as you made it. It's perfect.'

'Really?' she breathes hesitantly even as her face lights up. 'Better than a bed?'

I look at her, allowing myself to share the smile reserved only for her. 'Far better than a bed.'

She claps, and I'm no longer surprised by the action. Nor am I embittered by the joy that caused it. All I am is fortunate enough to witness it.

'Oh, good!' She sighs, sagging in relief. When I can do nothing but stare at it, she waves an insistent hand. 'Well, go on! Try it on!'

I oblige with little argument and swing the belt round me, buckling it quickly. It sits low on my hips, allowing easy access to the knives that will soon line it.

I shake my head in disbelief. 'This may be the only thing anyone has ever gotten me, but I'm quite certain nothing could be better.'

'That sounds like a challenge,' she remarks with a typical smile. 'The next gift will have to be even more spectacular.'

With a blank look, I state my rebuttal. 'Oh, there will be no more gifts.'

Making her frown like this would upset me if it weren't for such a ridiculous reason. 'And why not?'

I lean in, watching her eyes widen at my sudden closeness. 'Because I know how distraught you will be when nothing can compare to this.'

She twists a loose curl round her finger – an absentminded action I catch her doing often. 'We will see about that.'

'Dena,' I say softly, though it causes her head to whip up violently. 'Thank you.'

Her smile is sad. 'I'm sorry that I'm the first to give you a gift.'

'I'm not.' The words fall quickly from my lips. 'I would have waited another nineteen years if it meant you were the first good memory I was gifted.'

Hazel eyes wander up to mine. 'But you deserve more than one good memory.'

'Then it's a good thing I'm planning on keeping you around.'

She smiles at me, seeming to brighten the darkening alley around us. 'I would like that very much, Mak.'

The words have barely left her lips before a yawn

smothers them. I quirk an eyebrow. 'Tired?'

'Exhausted,' she says amidst another yawn. 'It is quite the workout walking down here from the castle.'

I scoff. 'Yeah, remind me to add endurance training to our fighting sessions.'

She groans, giving me a pleading look. 'And what will that be?'

I shrug before leaning back on my hands. 'I don't know. Make you run down the street a few times. Maybe dodge a couple of children.' A smile teases the corners of my mouth. 'That'll wear you out enough to lessen your word count in the evening.'

She crosses her arms defensively, her tone even more so. 'Well, maybe my word count and I should go elsewhere if we're unappreciated.'

'Oh, honey, it's more than appreciated. I dare say it's even admired.'

She swallows, looking sheepish. 'And that's why you barely look at me when I'm talking?'

I shake my head, thoroughly exasperated. 'Dena, if I looked at you while you were talking, I can't guarantee that I'd be paying attention to what you're saying.'

'Oh.' There's a long pause as she mulls this over. 'I see.'

Even in the spreading shadows, I can make out her

flustered features. She clears her throat a few too many times before slowly lowering her back onto the rough rug beneath us. After piling every blanket and scrap of fabric on top of her, she burrows beneath the cocoon of cloth.

A hand shoots out from beneath the mound, patting the space beside her. 'Lie down,' she insists. 'Here, I'll even share my blankets.'

I stiffen. 'I think something just moved beneath the rug.'

'Oh, it is so toasty under here!' Adena croons over my concern.

'Yeah, stay there so whatever is crawling around will burrow in there with you.'

Before I have a chance to run away, she's tugging me by the weapons belt. I'm lying beside her in a heartbeat, unsure of how I found myself in this very unpleasant position.

'See, it's not so bad!' I can hear the smile in her voice and do not bother to return it.

'Sure, if you enjoy restless sleep.'

Her body wiggles closer to mine, pressing a bare shoulder against my thinly clothed one. The heat of her thoroughly warms me, even managing to spread up to my cheeks. She feels suddenly delicate beside me, and the urge to wrap a protective arm round her is difficult to shake.

'I count the stars,' she says softly. 'To help me sleep.'

I roll my head towards her, watching her silhouette stare up into the sky. Awe laces each word from her soft lips. 'I always wondered how something could shine so bright, even while being swallowed in darkness.'

My eyes run over the shadowed outline of her face. 'I've been trying to figure that out myself.'

'I hope they know how admired they are up there,' she murmurs. 'I mean, I count them before bed every night.'

I shake my head at the sight of her admiring something far duller than her.

'I'm quite sure that even the stars are envious of you.'

Her head turns towards me, pulling her eyes from the sky and pinning them on me. 'What?'

'You make even the stars envious,' I repeat softly, leaning towards her. 'Because one day – far from now – you will be up there beside them, outshining every single one.'

I'm not sure what it is about her that has me suddenly spewing prose like a poet, but if I've learned anything from her, it is to no longer hide what it is I'm feeling. Even if that means admitting things I likely shouldn't.

I can feel her quick breaths, practically hear her racing thoughts. Every inch of her is tense against me, and when my knuckles brush hers, air catches in her throat. After several shaky breaths, she whispers, 'And will you be beside me up there?'

'If I should be so lucky.'

'Promise me,' she murmurs sternly. 'I don't want to be alone.'

I nod against her hair. 'I promise, Dena.'

CHAPTER 16

Adena

'I have my next gift for you.'

Plopping down on his bed, I clutch the surprise behind my back and watch him stride towards me. Ash clings to his hands and bleeds up his arms. My eyes run over the strands of black hair falling in his face above the shirt that clings tightly to his body. I swallow at the sight of him but force my flustering to a minimum.

His long legs reach me in a matter of moments. 'I thought we decided on no more gifts. For your own sanity.'

'You decided that.' I shrug. 'I decided to try to top the last one.'

'You should know that I'm justifiably frightened.'

'It's nothing bad, I swear!' I gesture to the empty mattress beside me. 'All right, take a seat.'

The bed groans as he slowly sinks into it. 'Now,' I insist slowly, 'close your eyes.'

He sighs before obeying. 'Yes, very frightened.'

Ignoring him, I lift the gift between us, displaying it over my outstretched arms. 'Okay, open!'

He peeks at me through his lashes, ensuring it's safe before opening them fully. But once he has, his jaw follows, gaping slightly in awe.

'It's different to the vest I made Pae,' I say hurriedly. 'For starters, it's black instead of green. I figured that was more your color.' Draping the vest carefully in his arms, I point to the pockets lining it. 'And yours is lined with more of that leftover leather, so you can stick some knives in there and without worrying about being stabbed!'

He shakes his head, running ash-stained fingers over each seam. 'How are you so good?'

'Well, Mama ensured I could stitch a straight line with my eyes closed, and pockets took some practice but—'

'No,' he cuts in softly, his laugh equally so. 'You.

How can one person be so good?'

The corner of my mouth tugs into a timid smile. 'It's not very hard when you've been practicing your whole life.'

He's looking at me in that way he often does. As though he's laying eyes on me for the first time, discovering something entirely foreign to gaze at. It's this look that makes me feel as though I'm the only thing that has ever captured his attention.

Too soon, his gaze falls. His fingers dance over the fabric, faltering beneath one of the pockets. 'What's this?'

I smile sheepishly. 'Oh, I left you a message.'

His eyes flick to mine before skimming over the embroidered purple thread. I've never been much good with my lettering, but the cursive is clean enough to read, at the very least.

'See you in the sky,' he murmurs, running his finger over the sentence and the accompanying stars I stitched beside it. His smile grows as he says, 'Seems a little ominous, don't you think?'

'Not if you think of it fondly,' I say simply.

'You are quite the oddity, Dena.'

My smile is achingly large. 'Why, thank you.'

'No.' He's suddenly stoic. 'Thank you, honey. I'll wear it fondly.'

Our eyes lock for several slow seconds before I finally let the question slip out. 'Why do you call me that?' At his raised brow, I elaborate with a hurried, 'Honey?'

'I thought it was obvious.' He shrugs, seemingly indifferent. 'You are what you eat.'

I'm rendered speechless by this, and he takes the opportunity to continue. But only after he's inched closer, filling me with warmth at the mere press of his body. I think I stop breathing when his hand lifts, slowly making its way towards my face.

I watch his throat bob as he brushes the bangs from my eyes, tickling my skin with the whisper of fingers. His breath stirs my hair, awakening the butterflies in my stomach, slicking the palms in my lap. Knuckles brush down the length of my cheek, and I'm too enthralled to wonder whether he's left a trail of ash across my skin. When he speaks, I swear it's to my very soul. 'You are the sweetest thing I have never tasted.' Another brush of his knuckles. 'And I doubt I've craved anything more.'

Holy shit.

I'm not one for profanity, but my current situation

seems to warrant it. I want to scream it, duck beneath his arm and run until I hit the Scorches. But I'm rooted to the spot, knee-deep in mutual feelings I hadn't dreamed could be this vast.

And it terrifies me.

I've never been someone's. And I have no idea how to be.

I'm so scared of doing it wrong, that I'm considering not doing it at all.

His feelings for me were reserved for daydreaming and delusional thinking. We were a fantasy I constructed in my head, wondering for weeks if it would ever become reality. And now that it has—

'Plagues, these bangs!' I jump away from his tempting touch, laughing nervously. 'They are just always in my eyes – drives me crazy!'

He blinks at me, trying to interpret my sudden outburst. Fanning my hot face with a hand, I ramble on. 'Pae usually cuts my bangs for me, which is why they are so crooked. Well, she likes to think it's because I move around while she's cutting, but I beg to differ. And she's been so busy lately, so now they are long enough to continually stab me in the eyes—'

'I'll cut them.'

His words startle me into silence for several seconds. 'You . . . You would do that?'

He scoffs in the sweetest way possible. 'I practiced my skipping for you. This is nothing.'

Before I can stammer a response, he stands to dig around in a nearby cabinet. He's then striding back to me, dusty scissors in hand. Sinking into the mattress beside me, he lifts the blades towards my face.

I lean away, laughing anxiously. 'Okay, um, have you ever done this before?'

'Cut hair? No.' His voice is flat. 'But I have plenty of experience in cutting things.'

'Great.' I squirm when the scissors grow closer.

'All right, if you keep that up, I'll stab you in the eye.' The look of horror on my face must urge him to say, 'No, not on purpose.'

'Okay, okay.' I take a deep breath. 'I am calm and definitely not scared right now.'

'That is convincing enough for me,' he says, sarcastically cheery.

The first snip of hair has me biting my tongue. By the third, I'm giggling.

He sighs. 'What now?'

'Nothing,' I snort. 'Just tickles.'

'Paedyn was right. These crooked bangs are all your doing.'

I cross my arms, attempting to sit still. 'Maybe I like my bangs a little crooked. Adds character.'

'Oh, you don't need any more of that.'

He makes the final cut, letting the hair fall into my lap alongside the rest. I collect the ends of my curls into a palm, silently mourning their loss as though they felt each cut of the blade.

When I look back up at him, he slowly raises a hand towards me, giving me enough time to duck away. But instead, I still, allowing him to run his fingers through the freshly cut bangs.

'Still crooked?' I ask quietly.

He nods, smiling with the corner of his mouth. 'Not if you tilt your head.'

The sorrow in his gaze has lessened with each passing day, and when I look at him now, all I see is contentment. Acceptance. I grin back, nodding to his shiny hair and each strand escaping the hastily tied strap. 'Well, not all of us can have perfect hair.'

He laughs, and I shudder at the deep sound of it. 'My hair is probably the least perfect thing about me.' He gestures to the streak of silver peeking out amongst the black strands. 'It's marred by this streak of . . .'

His voice trails off when my fingers find that strip of silver. I trace the strands, memorize the feel of it beneath my fingertips. I can hear him breathing, feel him inching closer with each passing second.

'I think it's perfect,' I whisper, smiling at the shining silver. 'Like my little piece of Pae.'

His hand finds my waist, fingers firm in a way that has my head spinning. Right when I think I may combust at his touch, that hand of his begins traveling up my back to tug me towards him.

He pulls me close, and I'm suddenly, silently hoping he never stops. With his arm wrapped tightly round me, he leans forward until our foreheads brush. And that's when he whispers, 'I think you're my little piece of perfection.'

My heart pounds at his words, at the feel of his hold and brush of his fingers.

I've spent my whole life wishing to be wanted. And here he is, begging me to let him.

I pull back just far enough to meet his eyes, finding reverence in his gaze. With a deep breath, all fear seems to fall away when I focus on him. When I abandon expectations and simply *am*.

He is my fantasy. This is my reality.

With that realization, all hesitation vanishes.

And I kiss him.

My hands cup his face, fingers splayed over proud cheekbones. It's light, this kiss. Innocent and sweet. He kisses me gently, holds me protectively. His lips are soft against mine, tender and warm.

I pull back slightly, eyeing him through the bangs he just cut. But his gaze is on my lips, tracing the shape of them. The sight of it has my heart pounding wildly, my mind murmuring ideas that I've never had the courage to carry out before this moment.

His hand flexes against my back, forcing me to take a shaky breath. 'I . . . I'm not very good at this, Mak,' I stammer breathlessly. 'I'm not used to the boys I like actually talking to me, let alone touching me like—'

'Are you going to stop talking long enough to let me kiss you properly?' His voice is breathless, eyes flicking down to my lips.

'Um . . .' I swallow, inching towards him. 'Well, I haven't quite met my word count for the—'

His lips crash into mine.

This kiss is quite the opposite of the first one we shared. His hands are in my hair, running down my neck. It is deep and drawn out and everything I've ever dreamed of.

He drops an arm round my waist, pulling me tight enough against him that I vaguely wonder if he can feel my thundering heart. Before I can talk myself out of it, I've swung a leg over both of his, finding myself suddenly perched on his lap.

He does something then. Something far more intimate than any kiss or touch so far. No, he pulls back far enough to let me see him smile.

It's big and bright and beautifully his.

'For me?' I ask breathlessly, staring at his smile.

'Every single one,' he murmurs.

I kiss him fiercely. I kiss him the way I've fantasized kissing someone my whole life. I kiss him like it's the end of a fairy tale.

A calloused hand cups my face while the other roams over my back. His lips move against mine as he breathes me in. And I gladly let him. Would gladly be more than a piece of his perfection. I could fill him completely, stuff him with my sentiment until he's sick on it.

I would give him every piece of me if he only asked politely.

I pull back, breathing heavily.

Mak does the same, tipping his forehead against mine. A confession crawls up my throat, tearing at my sealed lips before finally spilling out. 'I'm tripping into you, Mak.'

His thumb brushes across my cheek. 'Tripping into me?'

I nod, breath shaky. 'I don't fall for someone. I trip uncontrollably towards them before inevitably hitting the ground.'

He smiles softly, the action delicate atop his stern features. His eyes wander over my face while his fingers tuck unruly hair behind my ear. 'Well, I would catch you, Dena, but it seems we're going down together.'

I blink at him, my smile widening. 'Really?'

He nods slowly. 'Really.'

I press my lips together, trying to hide my giddiness. I quickly fail and, instead, press a kiss to his lips. It's a struggle to pry myself away from him after several seconds too long.

'I have to go back to the castle tonight.' My words fade into a giggle when he circles his arms round my waist, capturing my lips once again. I laugh against his mouth, barely able to get my next sentence out. 'I still have to finish up—'

Another kiss cuts me off.

'—Pae's dress for—'

I initiate this kiss.

'—the ball tomorrow,' I finish with a dizzying smile.

I manage to climb from his lap before he can stop me. With my cloth bag quickly slung over my shoulder, I head for the door. Mak is on my heels, closing his arms around me from behind.

Giggling, I place my arms atop the ones he's wrapped round my waist. 'I was right,' I say cheerily, 'you're not half as grumpy as you seem.'

I feel him straighten behind me. 'Yeah, shit, what did you do to me?'

I laugh, turning to face him. 'I'll see you tomorrow evening.' I jab a finger in his face. 'At the Fort, remember?'

'Oh, so I won't be sleeping.' He smiles sarcastically. 'Can't wait.'

I roll my eyes before teetering up on my toes to peck him on the cheek. He smiles sweetly, his cold exterior melting within a matter of moments.

When he suddenly lifts the hem of his shirt towards my face, I open my mouth to spew a question he's already answering. 'There's ash on your face, hun. That might be my fault.'

I beam up at him until he's finished cleaning my skin. And then I kiss him goodbye, soft and sweet.

'I'll see you soon,' I whisper.

'I'm counting down the hours, Dena.'

CHAPTER 17

Adena

My arms are draped in darkness.

Black fabric spills over my hands as I scurry out of the sewing room. I smile down at the silky gown, unable to contain my giddiness at the sight of it.

This may be my most beautiful creation yet, and I can't think of a more beautiful person to do it justice.

The halls are bustling with staff, all preparing for the final ball looming far too close. With that in mind, I pick up my pace, dodging a parade of Imperials heading for the ballroom.

I wasn't there for that first ball – or the second, for that matter – seeing that I was snuggled with Mak in

the Fort. But I heard of the attack, nonetheless. Ever since, the number of Imperials crawling around has greatly increased. I shudder despite the extra sense of safety they provide.

Plush carpet softens my steps, and I'm suddenly distracted by the feel of it. I can only imagine how impossible it would be to wake Pae up if the rug beneath our Fort was this comfortable. But if she manages to win these Trials, our first order of business will be to find something equally as soft—

My arms collide with a very solid someone.

Eyes flying up from the floor, I meet the equally distracted gaze above me. It's gray and stormy and – Plagues help me – it belongs to Prince Kai.

I stumble into a curtsy, clutching the silky gown against my chest before it has the chance to slip between my sweaty palms. 'Prince Kai! I didn't even see you there! This carpet is terribly distracting.'

For once, I snap my mouth shut before I can do any more damage. When my gaze finally lifts from his black tunic, I'm relieved to find an amused expression on his face.

Plagues, he's pretty.

I hope he doesn't see the physical shake of my head as

I attempt to expel the thought from it. Because I have a pretty boy of my own. Though, I can admit that Pae is quite a lucky woman.

The corner of his mouth tips upward. 'You must be Adena.'

'Yes?' I answer, confusion curling the word into a question. 'How do you...' I step aside for a scurrying servant. 'How do you know that?'

'Well, there is only one girl in this castle daring enough to wear anything but green to the ball tonight.' He runs those gray eyes over the draped fabric in my arms. 'So that would make you her seamstress from Loot.'

I blink up at him. 'Um, yes, it would.' With a smile, I add, 'You are quite observant!'

His gaze flicks over the fabric. 'I've been spending a lot of time with your Psychic friend.'

I bite my tongue.

It is incredibly odd to be in on the ruse that everyone else believes. But I smile at him, nonetheless, honored to keep Pae's secret. 'Oh, I know.' My eyes widen. 'I mean, that is great to hear, Your Highness!'

There's that slight smirk again. 'She's picked black tonight, then.'

I glance down at the gown. 'She certainly has. And I have no doubt that she will look stunning.'

'Neither do I,' he says smoothly. 'She will certainly be turning heads, though, that's no surprise.'

Eyeing him closely, I select my words carefully. For once. 'So, you're okay with her not wearing green?'

He barely considers my question. 'Of course. I wouldn't want her to blend in.'

A small smile lifts my lips as I take in the future Enforcer. He certainly is not his brother. No, it seems that Kai would prefer Paedyn make a statement. Stand out.

And just like that, I've picked which pretty prince to root for. Because it's Kai who is destined for Paedyn, no matter how tragic their story. No matter the opposite roles they play in this life. But maybe things will be different in the next.

'That is good to hear,' I say quietly.

He's sloppily rolling up the sleeves of his tunic, saying, 'Why did it distract you?'

'I'm sorry?'

He nods to our feet. 'The carpet.'

'Oh!' I shrug, struggling to select which words I wish to say. 'I was trying to memorize the feel of it beneath my feet. So Pae and I can get a rug this plush for our Fort.'

Emotion flits across his face, though I can't seem to decipher it. The dark lashes lining his light eyes flutter and, for a moment, it looks as though he may say something. Instead, he takes a step away, ending our conversation with a single movement. Nodding curtly, he says, 'I hope you find that rug.'

Then he turns, tossing a smirk over his shoulder. 'You'll get to her room much faster if you phase through the wall. Trust me, I've done it plenty of times.'

And with that, the Enforcer strides down the crowded hallway, Imperials parting for him.

I blink, bewildered, at his back. It's suddenly difficult to swallow.

How could I have forgotten what he is?

I've just met Mak's equal. The man who could have him killed in an instant. All because they possess the same power. And it seemed to roll off the prince in waves – so at odds with the Wielder hidden within Loot. Though they felt eerily familiar, both foreboding in their own ways.

I shake my head, mind buzzing as I once again begin my journey down the bustling hall, but I stop short at the sight of the wall beside me.

I might as well take his advice.

Stepping out onto the other side of the wall, her bedroom awaits mere paces away. I sigh in relief when I'm finally whipping open her door. 'Pae, I hope you're prepared for all the attention you'll be getting in this dress!'

Her head peeks round the dressing screen, silver hair swishing with the movement. 'I really hope you're exaggerating.'

I hurry over to where she hides, finding Ellie exasperated by the amount of hair she has to deal with. But this is a recurring problem that I don't feel the need to fret about.

Instead, I unravel the dress, displaying it against my body. 'You tell me,' I say, my smile smug. 'Do you think this will get even the royals staring? Especially one in particular?'

Pae gapes at the gown before her, coal-lined eyes running over the length of it. 'I'm afraid it will.'

'Perfect!' I shrug contently. 'Then I've done my job well.'

'Adena,' Pae scoffs, even with a look of awe lighting her face. 'You may have done your job a little too well.'

'Why, are you worried a certain prince may fall to his knees at the very sight of you?' I say dreamily.

Pae's cheeks redden even as she crosses her arms and says, 'I have no idea what you are talking about, A.'

I tap a finger to my lips. 'Hmm. Well, his name rhymes with "eye" . . .'

'And "guy",' Ellie chimes in softly.

My face lights up. 'Oh, and I might have just talked to him in the hallway.'

She whips round so fast that I narrowly miss inhaling a mouthful of silver hair. 'You did not.'

I sigh, smiling blissfully. 'I did.'

'What could you two possibly have talked about?' she says, exasperated.

'Hmm, let me think. What common interests could we have?' I smile wickedly. 'Oh, that's right. You!'

Ellie giggles while Paedyn stifles a groan. 'Plagues, maybe I'd rather not know.'

'Well, to sum it all up,' I continue anyway, 'he agreed that you would look stunning tonight. And he will definitely want to dance with you.'

I press my lips together. Those words didn't exactly leave his mouth, but Pae doesn't need to know that. And, besides, I'm sure he was thinking it.

Pae sighs, spinning that ring on her thumb incessantly. 'Don't remind me.'

I frown. 'Did something happen?'

She laughs humorlessly. 'Too much happened.'

I help peel off her remaining clothing before she steps into the dress. 'Oh, do tell,' I say, greedy for every detail.

She slips her arms through the dainty sleeves that lay limply around her arm. 'Can I fill you in after the Trial, A?' She sounds exhausted. 'I'm still trying to process it all myself.'

I help her tug the corset up. 'Of course, Pae. You need to focus on the Trial.'

I say this to ease my guilty conscience. I have yet to tell her of Mak and every moment I've spent with him. She knows of my tendency to trip for someone, and yet, she will be one of the last to know.

'Thanks, A,' Paedyn smiles, looking relieved.

'Don't thank me yet.' I wiggle a finger, gesturing for her to turn around. 'I haven't tightened the corset.'

'Plagues,' she murmurs. 'If this dress was any less beautiful, I might beg not to wear it.'

'Oh, please,' I tease. 'You love dressing up, even if you won't admit it. Isn't that right, Ellie?'

'I mean . . .' Ellie hesitates. 'You do seem to enjoy it . . .'

Pae's scoff is cut short when I tug at the laces of her corset. 'Well, I sure as hell don't enjoy being unable to breathe.'

'But you're breathtaking.' I attempt to smother my snort. 'Quite literally.'

'I think you're enjoying this a little too much, A,' she gasps.

'This may be my last chance to dress you up.' I tighten the laces, earning a grunt from Pae. 'So I might as well take advantage of it!'

After much pleading from Pae, I finally tie off the laces of her corset and spin her round to admire my work. Most of the bodice is see-through, showing off her tan skin beneath the beads and swirling pattern decorating the corset. The sleeves are dainty and purely for design, as they do nothing to keep the dress up from where they dangle off her shoulders.

My eyes take in the pooling skirt and the matching slits on either side. As I do so, Paedyn pushes the fabric apart to strap her silver dagger high on a thigh. Then she straightens, standing before Ellie and me for inspection. 'So? What do you think?'

'You look beautiful, Paedyn,' Ellie breathes with a smile.

Unwanted tears prickle my eyes at the vision before me. 'You look dangerous. But in the most elegant of ways.'

She seems to melt at my words. 'That may be the best compliment I've ever received.'

Ellie sighs. 'You need to head to the ballroom soon, and I still have no idea what to do with your hair.'

'Something simple,' I suggest. 'Maybe an updo? I want to see those collarbones of hers.'

Ellie obliges, tying Pae's hair into a loose knot at the back of her neck, allowing strands to fall around her face as they please.

I clasp my palms in front of me, beaming at the finished product. 'Gorgeous! Now go before you're late!'

Paedyn laughs lightly, reaching out to squeeze my hands. 'Thank you, A. I can't tell you how much I love each of the dresses you've made for me.'

'I knew you loved them,' I say slyly. 'And me, of course.'

'And you.' She grins. 'Of course.'

My smile suddenly fades into something far more serious. 'Promise you'll make it back to me after this Trial?'

'I promise I'll try my absolute hardest,' she murmurs

earnestly. 'Just one more, and I'm free. *We* are free.'

My lips lift into an unexpected smile. 'I'll be cheering you on the whole time, Pae.'

We admire one another for a long moment before I begin shooing her towards the door. 'All right, go dance with your prince!'

'Not if I can help it!' she calls, throwing a smile over her shoulder before disappearing down the hallway.

Ellie turns to face me as soon as she's out the door. 'You off to go see your boy?'

I beam. 'That I am.' Gathering up my cloth bag, I stride to the door with a blissful smile. 'I'll be back for the Trial tomorrow, don't worry. Even though I'm not sure how much I'll be able to stomach watching.'

After returning Ellie's wave goodbye, I step out into the hallway and smother the urge to skip with excitement. I buzz with anticipation of our night at the Fort and—

And someone steps in my path.

It's a servant. He's young and timid and looking up at me uncertainly. 'Oh!' I exclaim. 'Hello there.'

But he doesn't return my politeness. No, he only offers me a single, rehearsed line.

'The king has requested to speak with you this evening.'

CHAPTER 18

Makoto

I'm shockingly happy as I head towards the Fort.

I can't remember the last time I was this happy, even with Hera.

Hera.

It feels wrong to be enjoying life with her no longer in it, but I still mourn her every day, in any way I can. I see her in the smiling faces along the street, remember how her magic tricks used to be the reason for laughing children and enthralled parents. I hear her in the sharpening of a blade for how she used to beg me to let her do it when we were young. I smell her in the rain, a brewing storm.

She's all around me, and yet, nowhere to be found.

I mourn alone. Quietly. Though I allowed myself a single night to break down in Adena's arms.

But Hera is likely already forgotten by the people, just another victim of the Trials she had no chance of winning. I try not to ponder the part I played in her death or my failed attempt to save her.

It hurts too much. To think I fumbled her freedom. Our freedom.

I could never leave now. Not with Adena still here.

I elbow through the crowded street beginning to close for the evening. Bits of dull conversation fill my ears as I head for the familiar dead end.

I can't help but smile at the sight of her colorful banner as it waves welcomingly at me. Something about it feels so like her. So comforting. So innocent and sweet.

Though she certainly didn't kiss me that way.

Well, at first, maybe. But then she quickly met my demand.

The way her mouth moved against mine was hypnotic. And if she had asked anything of me in that moment, I fear I would have had no choice but to do it.

Stepping over the barrier, I take a seat on my borrowed side of the rug. I feel dirtier by the second.

Paedyn need not worry about me permanently stealing her spot.

The thought flows into another, and I'm suddenly wondering if Adena has even told her best friend about me. But that thought quickly escalates to the more troubling one being that Adena has *truly* told her best friend about me. About my power. And the whole kingdom is buzzing about how close the contestant and future Enforcer have gotten over the course of these Trials. All it would take is a single slip of her words and the prince would know what I am—

I shake the trail of increasingly worrisome thoughts away. I've been ensured that Dena is a great secret keeper. Though, I have no sources to back up this claim.

I fidget on the rug, trying my best not to touch anything. Waiting impatiently for Adena to arrive, I pull the slim box from one of the many pockets on the vest she made. The lid slides off easily, allowing me to admire what lies within.

The needle is slightly larger than the ones I've witnessed her stab each finger with. The silver gleams, even in the dull light. I'm just able to make out the intricate, half-moon designs carved across the length of it.

I've never gotten a gift for someone. Not like this, anyway.

Not something that is filled with affection, given out of wanting rather than necessity.

And that's the terrible truth of it. I want her.

What did she call it? Tripping into me?

I stare at glinting needle, as though it could summon her to the alley and my awaiting arms. Because somewhere along the way, I started my trip into her. And now there is no stopping my violent careen.

Time ticks by, dousing the alley in darkness. I've covered my gift for her, stowing it safely back in my pocket. My eyelids grow heavy with my back slumped against the grimy wall.

Where is she?

I doubt she would miss our night in the Fort unless absolutely necessary. She likely got busy with Paedyn. Maybe forced to help with some fashion emergency.

I smile at the thought. She's probably having the time of her life telling people what to wear and how to wear it.

I sigh, gathering my legs beneath me to stand.

She got busy, I'm sure of it. And she will profusely apologize to me for simply doing her job. I'll tell her that she owes me a kiss. Maybe two. Maybe a dozen.

On the bright side, I don't have to sleep in the Fort.

Stepping out onto the deserted street, I begin weaving my way back to the shop. I catch sight of a crooked flyer dressing a nearby wall and struggle to skim over it in the darkness.

To no one's surprise, it's about the final Trial taking place tomorrow. I roll my eyes bitterly, ready to enjoy a blissful five years before these Trials come back to haunt us again.

My eyes stumble over the large sentence scrolled in the very center of the flyer.

'This year's final Trial will take place in the Bowl Arena – all are welcome and encouraged to watch.'

Now, this wouldn't mean shit if it were any other year. The Trials are typically held in the Bowl for the kingdom's entertainment. But this year has been different. This year, they have yet to compete within the arena.

I'm about to dismiss it when I remember who is going to be there.

Adena.

She will be in those stands, watching over her best friend between the fingers covering her eyes. I've never dared enter the Bowl for any Trial in the past, but I had also never had her.

I could surprise her. Sit with her. Comfort her.

It's dangerous, but it's for Dena.

I'll walk her back to the Fort – that alone will be a surprise. And then I'll give her the gift still securely in my pocket. She'll squeal, and I'll smile, just for her.

I turn down the alley that leads to my shop when a smile threatens to tip my lips.

Because for the first time in my life, I'm excited to go to a Trial.

CHAPTER 19

Adena

I *may never see him again.*

Never see that smile that sneaks out when we are together. Never see that vest that hugs him tightly, just as I wish to right now. Never see that silver streak of hair I find so comforting.

Never see if we trip into love together.

But, worst of all, I may never get to apologize for missing our date at the Fort.

It is cold in the dungeons.

I suppose that's to be expected. Not that I had planned on experiencing it firsthand anytime soon.

The damp wall pressed against my back has me wishing I'd been wearing a sweater when the king summoned me. Or perhaps my cardigan with the lace trim. Though I'd hate to wear it for the first time to the dungeons, with no one but the occasional Imperial to admire my handiwork.

I shut my eyes against the lone, flickering light beyond my bars and lean a throbbing temple against the stone wall. My stomach has been far chattier than anyone down here, growling with my growing hunger. I peek open an eye to stare at the stale bread tossed carelessly in the corner of my cell. After wincing at the mere thought of moving, I'm viciously biting my tongue as I shift closer. The shackles clamped round my ankles have my eyes stinging, skin tearing like sheer fabric. Rusty metal has rubbed my skin raw, leaving angry red blisters beneath.

Taking a shaky breath, I reach for the bread.

I know what I'll see. I even squeeze my eyes shut to prolong the inevitable, to pretend this is all a nightmare that Pae will wake me up from. Because she always did. She always found a way to fight off fear, to be strong enough for the both of us. I would feel the brush of her fingers against the uneven bangs I made her cut for me, and the soothing touch was enough to drag me from my dreams. And then we would sit with my head on her shoulder, staring at the stars until they melted into morning.

But this is not the Fort. And there are no stars in sight or shoulders to rest my pounding head on. I am very much awake and opening my eyes and—

The sight of my fingers has me swallowing a sob. I wish they had bound my hands behind my back, if only so I couldn't look at them.

I'm not sure why they did it. Or, better yet, why I'm down here in the first place.

I screamed when they began breaking my fingers, pleaded despite the pain, begged them to spare the one thing I loved to live for. My fingers are my craft, my comfort, my connection to the past I've managed to survive.

And then I cried.

It was a silent sort of mourning at first, tears slipping from behind squeezed eyelids. But my composure has never been anything to brag about. It wasn't long before I was sobbing at the sound of my cracking bones and broken dreams.

It's only when my outstretched hand grows blurry

that I realize I'm crying. Again. It seems that's all I've done since the king ordered me thrown in here. Why is that again? I still haven't puzzled that one out quite yet. Although, I have been rather occupied.

Sniffling, I strain towards the bread, sucking in a breath when the chains round my ankles grow taut. The pain of it all is too much. I'm not like Pae. I'm not used to hurting so heavily. I'm used to pricked fingers and sore hands, not an aching body and broken bones.

I huff and slump against the wall.

It's no big deal, really. I'm used to being hungry. In fact, I don't even want the stale bread.

My stomach protests. Very loudly.

I'm about to remind it that we've suffered longer without food, and to not be so dramatic, when the shadows begin speaking. How very odd.

'Would ya keep it down over there? I'm tryin' to sleep.'

I startle at the gruff voice and squint into the cell beside me. 'I-I didn't say anything.' My own voice is hoarse, scratchy like wool.

'Yeah,' the man grumbles, 'well, your stomach sure as hell has a lot to say.'

'Yes,' I sigh. 'All of me is quite chatty.' My eyes trace

the faint outline of a figure tucked into the corner connected to my cell, the corner closest to that dreadful bread. And he might just be able to reach it for me. 'I'll tell you what,' I begin cheerily. 'If you toss me that bread, my stomach will quiet down. So, we'll both get what we want. I'll eat, you'll sleep.'

He seems to find this funny. Supposing, of course, that the noise coming from him is a laugh. 'Oh, yeah? And how d'you know I won't just take the bread for myself?'

'Well, are you in here for being a thief?'

'No. Worse.'

'Then I'll take my chances,' I say lightly. 'Sounds like you have no experience with thievery.'

He makes that noise again, the one I'm assuming is laughter. Then he's shifting, sliding bony fingers between the bars in search of my bread. After managing to grab ahold of it, he tosses the loaf over to me with a gruff grunt. It rolls, coming to a stop when it collides with my leg.

I smile into the shadows. 'See, you're no thief. Thank you.' I falter at the sight of my fingers. Twisted and broken and useless.

The pain is paralyzing.

I place a palm atop the loaf, wincing at the pressure. After a moment, I muster up the courage to press the bread between both hands and attempt to lift it towards my mouth. Tears slip down my cheeks. But I take a bite. And another. Each one stale and salty with my tears.

'Whatcha do, kid?' the voice asks, cutting through the sobs I'm choking down along with the bread.

'I . . .' A sniffle. 'I'm a seamstress. I-I used to be a seamstress.'

The ghost of a smile lifts my lips. 'Loot needs all the fashion help it can get. I had a whole little business. My best friend – she's actually in the Trials, you know. Well –' I frown – 'I guess you wouldn't know if you've been down here. Anyway, she would get me the fabric, and I would sew the clothes. Of course, I always made sure she had first call on anything I made. Oh, but I designed this vest for her with all these pockets, because, well, let's just say she did have experience with thievery—'

'No, kid.' He sounds annoyed. 'Damn, you sure do talk a lot, don't ya? I meant, whatcha do to end up down here?'

'Oh. Um. Your guess is as good as mine,' I say, struggling to swallow the tough bread between my teeth. 'Well, I did try to steal something once. It didn't end well. Pae is still shocked at how terrible a thief I am for being a Phaser.' I attempt another bite at the loaf. 'She always says that if she could walk through walls, she'd be unstoppable. And very rich.'

'What, they just throw you in here for no reason?' He snorts. 'It's not like you're an Ordinary or somethin'.'

The thought of this being Paedyn's fate has my stomach turning.

'No. No, I'm definitely an Elite. Not that it will help me any in here.' I glance at the stones surrounding the cells, feeling the Mute suppressing my powers so I can't simply phase through these bars.

Something about him feels suddenly serious. 'I wonder what they're gonna do to ya.'

'Well –' I lift my hands for him to see – 'there's not much worse they could do.'

'Yeah,' he says gruffly. 'I heard that happen.'

'Sorry for keeping you up, then,' I say halfheartedly. He chuckles at that, making me smile. 'Soooo,' I drag out the word, 'what did you do to end up down here, hmm?'

I can feel him watching me. 'Somethin' that earned me a spot in this dungeon. Unlike you.'

'People can change,' I say quietly.

'Not me.'

'I don't know about that,' I say cheerily. 'Helping a stranger out is probably the first step towards self-improvement.'

I don't know why, but it feels like he's smiling. 'What's your name, kid?'

'I'm Adena. But my friends – well, friend – call me A.' He grunts in response. 'What's your name?'

His tone is almost accusatory. 'Why you wanna know?'

I shrug. 'Maybe I'm trying to make another friend.' I'm not sure why he laughs at that. 'You don't wanna be friends with me, kid. They all end up dyin'.'

'Well, it sounds like you're in need of some more, then.'

Another rough chuckle. 'You make a good point, kid. Fine. I'm Al.'

'Al?' I repeat. 'Is that short for something?'

'Wouldn't know if it was.' He coughs, nearly choking. 'Never spoke to my parents. Just been on my own for as long as I can remember.'

'Hmm.' I'm quiet for a long moment, thinking briefly of how I never knew my father. My silence seems to unsettle him into speaking.

'Yeah, and I got no friends to give me a nickname.'

'Well –' I grin in his direction – 'you do now, A.'

'A?' he questions. 'Isn't that your nickname, kid?'

'From Pae, yes. From you, it sounds like you've settled on "kid".'

He laughs, the sound now making me smile. 'You're somethin' special, you know that, kid?'

I toss the rest of the loaf in his direction, watching his hand hesitantly pick it up. 'Thank you, A. I—'

Heavy footsteps echo off the dungeon walls, drowning out my words.

My cell door is swinging open before I'm suddenly swallowed by a swarm of Imperials. Two of them are yanking me off the ground, careless of my cracked fingers. I cry out, trying to shield my hands from them and—

Now I'm choking on something.

They've gagged me with what feels to be cotton. My protests are muffled as they drag me from the cell and into the hallway. I'm frantic, eyes wide as they meet Al's through the bars beside me. I can just make out his face now, crowded with wrinkles and covered with worry. He shakes his head at me, cowering in his corner.

All his friends end up dead. And I'm starting to think I'm not the exception.

He turns away from another doomed friend, growing blurry as my eyelids begin to flutter.

And then—

And then, nothing.

Blackness and blinding pain are all I know.

CHAPTER 20

Makoto

A parade of bodies lines the path to the Bowl.

The sun beats down on my bent head, slicking me with sweat. I look around, scanning the hundreds of Ilyans trudging from all directions. It seems that the entirety of the slums has come to see the outcome of this final Trial.

I feel the press of each power, weighing down my steps. Following the current, I blend in with the bodies surrounding us and continue the trek to the looming arena.

Under different circumstances, I would have only been walking for little more than an hour. But with this

crowd and the aggravating ability they possess to walk as slowly as possible, it takes much longer than that.

The sun is at its most scolding point in the sky by the time we file towards one of the many tunnels leading into the Bowl. The arena is coated in concrete, looking cold and uninviting. Conversations and footfalls echo off the arch of the tunnel we walk through before we are spit out onto the raised ring of pavement above the Pit floor.

Rows of seats rise towards the sky, filled with thousands of cheering Elites. The sheer size of this place is intimidating, let alone what is happening below us in the Pit. A giant maze of menacing hedges stretches across the sand, encircling a large opening in the center of it all.

I stand there, gawking at the arena as people brush past me in search of a seat. Only then am I reminded that I need to find one of my own and start striding further down the path.

'Not only do you have to be the first contestant to reach the middle . . .'

The source of this booming voice comes from a large glass box further down the path.

The king.

I swallow, feeling years of fear come rushing up my tightening throat. I always thought the day I saw the king would be my very last. But there's still time for that.

'. . . you must also kill the person that awaits you there,' he finishes, his eyes on the arena though irrationality has me worrying that they will find mine. But his words faze me least of all. I'm unsurprised by his willingness to sacrifice a criminal from his dungeons in order to put on a good show. Anything to up the stakes for his contestants.

The rest of his speech fades away as I focus on finding the one person I'm here for. Hundreds of powers buzz in my blood, and it's a struggle to suppress them in search of her. I haven't had much practice with the very ability I possess, seeing that I've been forced to hide it my entire life. So I hone in on the first, faint Phaser I can find.

My concentration shatters when the Trial begins with a ripple of shouts and slamming of feet against the floor. I watch as the contestants race into the thick foliage towards that center ring.

Shutting my eyes, I focus again on that Phaser ability. And, this time, when it tickles my skin, I latch onto it.

I follow the feel of it, eyes searching the stands as

I head down the path. It grows stronger, closer with every step.

That is, until it doesn't any longer.

The power hums faintly beneath my skin, and no matter how far I walk down the path, it never seems to get any stronger.

Before I know it, I've circled the entire arena, desperately trying to catch a glimpse of her bright smile in the crowd. Maybe a frantic wave of her hands when she sees me coming.

Nothing.

I stop suddenly, spinning around in the path. Confusion crawls up my throat to escape my mouth in the form of a frustrated sigh.

'Where the hell are you, Dena?' I mumble towards the stands stretching around me.

Maybe I've focused on the wrong Phaser. Maybe I'm not searching for my Adena, but someone else entirely.

So, I shut my eyes again, forcing myself to focus. But this power feels familiar, intimate. I'm drawn to it in a way that tells me it can only be her.

And it's tugging me to the right.

I peek open an eye, finding only the railing to the Pit beside me. I huff, shaking my head. Something is clearly wrong with me. Is the Mute that lines the stands messing with my ability to simply sense powers?

Trying again to feel her, I find myself quickly turning towards the railing once more.

I look out into the Pit, scanning the foliage and the live footage playing on the screens above it. A flash of silver hair tells me it's Paedyn who is currently being recorded running between the hedges.

There's that tug again.

My gaze sweeps over the scene, landing on the circle of sand at the center of it all.

There's a body there. Seemingly small and rightfully scared.

'. . . *you must also kill the person that awaits you there.*'

So this is the criminal who was unlucky enough to be thrown from the dungeons and into a far worse fate.

I blink at the figure.

And then my mouth goes dry.

I'm forced to clutch the railing in front of me to stop from sinking to my knees.

Because I know that dark hair, those curls that bounce with each terrified turn of her head.

I can make out those crooked bangs from where I stand.

My shout is swallowed by the roaring crowd.

I've found her.

At the center of a Trial.

CHAPTER 21

Adena

It is hot in the Pit.

Again, I suppose that's to be expected.

I wake to the sound of stomping feet. The chanting of thousands has my ears ringing as my senses slowly hum to life. After struggling to blink open my heavy eyelids, I startle at the sight of hedges looming around me.

Staggering to my feet proves to be rather difficult with my wrists now bound behind my back and my ankles bound beneath me. I gawk at the hedges surrounding me, gulp at the sounds coming from beyond the dense foliage. At least I don't have to look at my fingers anymore. Though they ache so badly that it's impossible

to forget what they look like. I do my best to ignore the image of cracked bones and swollen knuckles that persistently flashes in my mind.

I'm dreaming. I must be.

This is all just a nightmare. Pae will wake me soon with her fingers sweeping back my sweaty bangs. And then we will sit and stare at the stars from behind our Fort. Because that is where I am. That is where I want to be.

But that is not this place.

This place is hot sand beneath my bare feet and sun trickling down through the vines above my head. This place is a wall of greenery, a cage of foliage folding in on me. This place is foreign and familiar all at once.

My eyes widen with realization.

This place really is the Pit.

Why am I in the Pit? I can't possibly be in the Pit. Today must be the final Trial and—

Did I wake up in the final Trial? I couldn't have . . . I mean, why would I be . . . ?

I spin in a slow circle, struggling against the shackles binding my ankles together. My head is pounding from whatever it was that knocked me out, making my vision eerily hazy.

Thundering feet and growing cheers are my only indication that the Trial has begun.

So I stand there. Stunned and still and silently hoping this is all in my head.

Pae will find me. She'll know what to do. She always knows what to do.

Sweat rolls down my face. My fingers throb. My head aches. My stomach growls.

Time seems to slow. I hear a muffled scream and spin in its direction.

That terror couldn't have belonged to Paedyn. No, because she's strong and safe and probably standing right beyond these hedges, about to find me.

Patience has never been a quality I've possessed.

493.

I've started counting the seconds out of sheer boredom.

My legs are shaking, feeling unsteady beneath me.

494, 495, 496 . . .

I'm not sure what this Trial is supposed to be, but I'm pretty sure I have the worst seat.

It's difficult to ignore my throbbing fingers, or the nagging thought that I was thrown into this Trial for a reason.

What could they want with a useless seamstress?

521, 522, 523 . . .

Pae will win this. Her prize will be finding me.

Shouts echo from every direction, chanting names I can't make out.

Do they know I'm here? Do they see me struggling to stay standing?

The world begins spinning around second 547.

My mouth is so dry I can barely swallow.

552.

Any second now. She'll save me any second now.

The corners of my vision are creeping in on me, making it feel as though I'm looking through a long tunnel.

I just want to wake up so I can see the stars.

I'm so dizzy that I almost don't see the figure running towards me.

'Adena?'

Her voice cuts through the haze of pain. My Pae has found me.

She's bounding towards me, sand flying from her heels. I'm so flooded with relief that I sink to my knees, smiling at her blurry form. 'Paedyn!' I shout, attempting to stand. But the look on her face has me faltering.

Why does she look so upset? She's won.

Maybe I've worried her with my disappearance. The thought has me spewing an apology, frantically trying to make her understand where I've been. 'Pae, I'm so sorry. I—'

This second feels longer than all the ones prior.

This one feels like fire.

Fatal.

Like the beginning of the end.

Pain blooms in my chest, burns through my body.

I take my time looking down at what is to be the end of me.

I blink at the bloody branch that has found its way through my chest, vaguely wondering how it got there.

Everything feels dull, muted like the scream that tears from a throat that isn't mine.

My eyes slowly find their way to the girl sprinting towards me, watching the scream form on her lips but never hearing it leave them.

She catches me before I hit the sand. I'm being cradled in arms I wish I could feel. Fingers are brushing away my bangs, and I manage a smile at the familiar feeling.

She's always there to wake me from my nightmares, to push uneven bangs from my eyes.

I sense the pain racking my body rather than feel it. Like knowing when your heart has broken without needing to feel it shatter.

I keep my eyes on her. My strong Pae. She's telling me I'm going to be fine. I know I'm not.

I may be dying, but I'm not dumb.

She's promising me sticky buns now. Says she'll feed me so many that I'll grow sick of them. We both know that's a lie. My love for sticky buns will die with me.

Die.

What a silly word, one I typically associate with the color of my fabrics. How odd it is to assign three little letters to the end of my existence.

'. . . you have to promise me you'll stay—'

Her muffled words pierce me harder than the branch jutting from my chest. 'Pae.' I take a shaky breath. 'You know I don't make promises I can't keep.'

I don't hear much of what she says next. Her tears are splattering my face, though I can't feel them through the blanket of numbness smothering my body. She's just as stubborn as always, denying the death that is so obviously coming to claim me.

That is the one thing I do feel. The brush of Death's fingers down my face, like a calming caress. I thought

I would be frightened of him and the end he's dragging me towards. But it's comforting in a way, being fully aware that this is the end.

'Promise you'll wear it for me?'

The words slip from my mouth, blood quickly following. Through blurry vision, I see the question on her face more than hear it from her lips. 'The vest,' I choke out. 'Th–The green one with the pockets.' Death is shushing me, but I speak over him. 'The stitching took me ages, and I'd hate for all my . . . h–hard work to go to waste.'

It's the last piece of me left.

The last physical piece of my passion in life.

No. There's Mak. He is my passion in life. And I only wish for them both to wear my vests when I'm gone, tethering them to me for eternity.

But I say none of this.

She promises. She pleads. She pulls me closer.

She's so good. I'm not sure she knows how good she is. How her worth is so much more than what power is or isn't running through her veins.

I've never thought of her as anything less than extraordinary.

My eyelids grow heavy, but I force them open.

I'll have plenty of time to rest when I'm dead.

It's peaceful, being pulled into the unknown.

But leaving her is anything but.

I claw against Death, needing to speak one last time.

'This is not a goodbye . . . only a good way to say bye until I see you next.'

With numb lips, I leave her with that.

I wonder if I'll be able to watch over her when I get to wherever Death is taking me.

He better let me watch over her.

The taste of blood is bitter in my mouth, but the smile I muster for her is sweet.

And then I count.

One, two, three . . .

Death is gentle in a way life never was.

I look up into the sky, seeing stars swim in my vision.

What a beautiful night in the Fort.

Four, five, six . . .

I'm counting the seconds until I see her next.

I'm counting the stars until I see Mak shining beside me.

The stars wink at me, welcoming me home.

And on second eight, I know nothing.

CHAPTER 22

Makoto

My heart skips a few several beats, sputtering at the sight of her standing there in the sand.

I can't breathe, can't think, can't do anything but stare helplessly at her figure so far away.

This can't be right. Adena is the farthest thing from a criminal. The farthest thing from anyone who deserves to die.

An Imperial storms by, jostling my shoulder hard enough that I grab his arm. He whips round, temper flaring in his eyes. I've never once gone out of my way to interact with an Imperial, yet here I am, clutching his bicep and growling, 'She's not a criminal.

Why the hell is she in there?'

The man scoffs, shoving me away from him. And if I weren't so shaken, I likely wouldn't have let him. 'King's orders, slummer.' He bares his teeth in what he thinks is a menacing way. 'Grab me again and I'll throw you in there with her.'

'Well, in that case . . .' I catch his arm, twisting it out with a jerk that forces a gasp from his lips.

He staggers back, eyes wide with hatred. 'Why you—' He stops suddenly, and I fear the worst when his eyes narrow. 'On second thought, I think you'd be hurting far more if you simply watched her die.'

My chest heaves at his words, and before I can do something drastic, he spins on his heel and strides away. I'm left staring after him, breath shaky and palms sweaty.

I turn back slowly towards the arena, fearing what it is I'll find there. When my eyes land on her, I can just make out the rope binding her wrists behind her back.

But it's her fingers I focus on. They look wrong, oddly different to what I memorized from the many hours of watching her sew.

I squint, shading my eyes from the blinding sun.

And then I'm once again grasping the rail for support.

Her fingers are bent, swollen, broken behind her back.

Her sewing fingers. They have broken her sewing fingers.

Emotion clogs my throat, making it hard to swallow.

Those beautiful hands of hers. Those beautiful hands that have cupped my face, created countless pieces of clothing, clapped joyfully at the smallest of things.

And now they never will again.

I shake my head, fighting the tears that beg to fall.

No, this isn't happening. Why would this be happening to her?

A blur from the edge of the circle emerges from the foliage. Blinking away unshed tears, I lean over the railing, catching a glimpse of a vaguely familiar figure.

Paedyn.

Dangerously, I let hope grab ahold of my heart, forcing it to sputter back to life.

If what I know about her is true, then the Silver Savior would never hurt her other half. With that as my only hope, I watch her tear through the sand towards a stumbling Adena.

I pray to whatever will listen. Beg with every ounce of earnestness. Offer my life for hers.

And yet, it appears that nothing was listening. Nothing even cared enough to hear me out, consider my pleas.

Because a branch plunges into her back.

I scream.

The sound rips my throat raw, managing to turn hundreds of heads in my direction.

I can't look away, can't see anything but the blood blooming across her back. The branch pierces straight through her to protrude from her chest and the beautiful heart beating there.

When her knees hit the sand, mine meet the concrete.

Tears slide over my skin as I watch Paedyn fall to the ground beside her. Watch her cradle that head of curls, cling to her broken body.

It hurts to not be holding her. My heart aches and my vision blurs. The box in my pocket grows heavy against my chest, right above the mangled heart beating beneath.

The needle will never have the pleasure of being held by her.

And neither will I. Not ever again.

I can barely hear Paedyn's desperate shouts through the persistent ringing in my ears, but I keep my eyes trained on her, not daring to look away until she's truly left me forever.

Her eyes are trained on the sky. I picture those big hazel eyes that I loved to fall on me, and choose to remember them that way.

The Sights are now focused on her, displaying her death clearly on the screen above for all to see. I cover my mouth with a trembling hand, attempting to smother my sob.

She blinks slowly at the sky above, her eyelids growing heavier with each one.

She's counting the stars.

I break.

All of me. Every inch of my being shattering at the realization.

Sobs shake my body as I clutch the bars of the railing, my legs trembling atop the concrete.

It's a good thing I cut her bangs. The crooked strands kiss her forehead, allowing those hazel eyes clear view of the stars.

The stars she now counts for the last time.

I weep, unashamed, for her.

For the girl who shines so bright that the sun pales in comparison.

For the girl who I was helplessly tripping into.

For the girl who deserved a happy ending.

'Just count the stars, Dena.'

I choke out the words, whisper them on the wind that will carry her soul far away from me. 'Just count the stars.'

I count right along with her.

One, two, three . . .

Only, I'm counting down the seconds until I get to see her again.

Four, five, six . . .

I'll count until I'm up in the sky beside her.

Seven, eight, nine . . .

And I suddenly wish that second would come sooner.

Ten, eleven, twelve . . .

I feel her power flicker and fade.

And then I watch her die.

Watch the life drain from her dark skin, steal the light from her eyes.

The connection snaps. Her ability slips between my fingers. Leaving me cold and shaking without its comfort.

And I'll never feel it again. Never feel *her* again.

Thirteen, fourteen, fifteen . . .

When Paedyn's hand sweeps over her eyes, shutting out the world for eternity, I stand and stumble down the path with shaky legs.

Sixteen, seventeen, eighteen . . .

Tears blur my vision; anger burns my blood. I turn down a concrete tunnel leading to the world beyond. A world without her. A world she is no longer in.

And I'm not sure I can live in that world.

Nineteen, twenty, twenty-one . . .

My sobs echo off the walls, drowning out the cheers from inside the Bowl. It should have been me. I wish it was me.

Twenty-two, twenty-three, twenty-four . . .

They are cheering. Cheering as if a sliver of the sun hadn't just burned out before them.

Twenty-five, twenty-six, twenty-seven . . .

When my feet meet the path outside, and my face is thoroughly doused in sun, I fall to my knees once again.

I clutch the vest around me, pulling at the perfectly straight seams holding it together.

Twenty-eight, twenty-nine, thirty . . .

Never again will I get to admire her while she sews.

My head falls into my hands, collecting hot tears on

my palms. Then I'm running my fingers over the vest again, tracing every bit that her fingers graced.

Thirty-one, thirty-two, thirty-three . . . My heart stutters at the feel of raised thread beneath a pocket.

I don't need to look at it to know what it says. Don't need to read the words to have more tears rolling down my cheeks.

'See you in the sky.'

I look up, choking back a sob.

Thirty-four, thirty-five, thirty-six . . .

The sun drenches me in warmth, coats me in comfort. It's soothing. Gentle. Soft.

I smile sadly. Laugh despite the tears still staining my skin.

And there she is, outshining everyone.

In a way, she's always been the sun. Always the brightness that existed despite the presence of such darkness.

Thirty-seven, thirty-eight, thirty-nine . . .

'Thanks for picking the closest star, Dena.'

I take a shaky breath.

Forty, forty-one, forty-two . . .

'Looks like you'll be around to keep me company.'

CHAPTER 23

Adena

In the end, it was all light and dark, loud and soft.
I knew nothing but the memory of those I loved.
One, a friend. The other, unfinished.
And that alone is what I took with me into the next life.
But I watched, warm and bright and high above.
Just as he promised.

Turn the page for a sneak peek
of the second book in the epic
and sizzling Powerless trilogy
by Lauren Roberts

Coming July 2024

Rai

The halls are eerily empty at this hour.

Just as they are every year.

I take my time walking down them, stealing this sliver of peace for myself. Though stolen bliss is little more than smothered chaos.

I choose to ignore that thought as I turn down a dark hall, my footsteps soft atop the emerald carpet. A sleeping castle is comforting, solitude a rarity amongst royals.

Royal.

I almost allow myself to laugh at the title. I frequently forget who I was before what I became. A prince before

the Enforcer. A boy before the monster.

But, today, I am no one. Today, I simply get to be with who should have been.

A soft light leaks from beneath the doors of the kitchen. I manage a slight smile at the sight.

Every year. She's always here every year.

I gently push open the doors and step into the puddle of light cast by several flickering candles. The sweet smell of dough and cinnamon hangs in the air, swaddling me in warmth and memories.

'You're up earlier each time I see you.'

I meet Gail's smile with a small one of my own. Her apron is dusted with spices, her face streaked with flour. I lift myself onto the same counter I've sat atop since I was big enough to reach it – my palms flattened behind me, scars sticky from the countertop.

There's comfort in the normalcy of it all.

I smile at the woman who practically raised me, each grey hair a testament to the years she's spent putting up with the princes. I lift a single shoulder in a lazy shrug. 'Every year I sleep less.'

When her hands find her hips, I know she's fighting the urge to scold me. 'You worry me, Kai.'

'When have I not?' I say lightly.

'I'm serious.' She wags a finger, gesturing to the whole of me. 'You're too young to be dealin' with all this. It seems like only yesterday you were running around my kitchen, you and Kitt . . .'

She trails off at the mention of him, forcing me to resuscitate the dying conversation. 'I actually came from Father's—' I pause long enough to sigh through my nose – 'Kitt's study.'

Gail nods slowly. 'He hasn't left it since his coronation, has he?'

'No, he hasn't. And I wasn't in there long, either.' I run a hand through my disheveled hair. 'He was just informing me of my first mission.'

She's quiet for a long moment. 'It's her, isn't it?'

I nod. 'It's her.'

'And are you—?'

'Going to complete the mission? Do as I'm told? Drag Paedyn back here?' I finish for her. 'Of course. It's my duty.'

Another long pause. 'And did he remember what today is?'

I look up, nodding slowly as I meet her gaze. 'It's not his job to remember.'

'Right,' she sighs. 'Well, I only made one this year

anyway. Figured he wouldn't be able to join ya.'

'We'll cut him some slack.' With a nod, she adds, 'This is the first year he's missed, after all.'

She steps aside, revealing a glistening sticky bun beside the oven. I slide off the counter, smiling as I walk over to her. Only after I've kissed her on the cheek does she hand the plate to me.

'Now, go on,' she shoos. 'Go spend some time with her.'

'Thank you, Gail,' I say softly. 'For every year.'

'And the rest to follow.' She winks before shoving me towards the door.

I glance back at her, at this woman who was a mother to me when the queen could not be. She was warm hugs and affection, well-deserved scoldings and much-desired approval.

I fear where the Azer brothers would be without her.

'Kai?'

I'm halfway through the door when I stop to look back at her.

'We all loved her,' she says quietly.

'I know.' I nod. 'She knew.'

And then my feet are carrying me out into the shadowed hallway beyond.

The sticky bun sitting atop the plate in my hand is

tempting, smelling of cinnamon and sugar and simpler times. But instead I force myself to focus on walking the familiar path to the gardens, the same one I take this time each year from the kitchens.

It's not long before I'm heading for the broad doors that separate me from the gardens beyond. I barely glance at the Imperials standing guard or the ones sleeping uselessly beside them. The few who are awake pretend not to notice the sticky bun I'm carrying into the darkness with me.

I follow the stone path between the rows of colorful flowers I can't make out in the shadows. Statues covered in ivy litter the garden, several missing chunks of stone after taking one too many topples that certainly had nothing to do with me. The fountain ripples at the center of it all, reminding me of stifling days and understandable stupidity that had Kitt and me jumping into it.

But it's what sits beyond the garden that I'm here for.

I step out into the soft stretch of grass that was once layered with colorful rugs for the second Trial's ball. Not allowing myself to reminisce any further on that night, I follow the moonlight that strokes its pale fingers over the outline of her.

The willow tree looks hauntingly alluring, her leaves rustling in the soft breeze. I run my eyes over each drooping branch. Over each root breaking through the dirt. Every inch is beautiful and strong.

I push through the curtain of leaves to step beneath the tree I visit as often as life will allow it – but always on this day with a sticky bun in hand. I run my fingers along the rough bark of the trunk, following its familiar grooves.

It's not long before take my usual seat beneath the towering tree, draping an arm over my propped knee. Balancing the plate atop a particularly large root, I pull a small matchbox from my pocket.

'I couldn't find a candle this year, sorry.' I strike the match, staring at the small flame now sputtering on the stick. 'So this will have to do.'

I push the match into the center of the sticky bun, smiling slightly at the pathetic sight. I take a moment to watch it burn, watch it paint the massive tree in a flickering glow.

Then I look down beside me, running a hand over the soft grass there.

'Happy birthday, A.'

I blow out the makeshift candle out, letting darkness swallow us whole.

CHAPTER 1

Paedun

My blood is only useful if it can manage to stay inside my body.

My mind is only useful if it can manage not to get lost.

My heart is only useful if it can manage not to get broken.

Well, it seems I've become utterly useless, then.

My eyes flick over the floorboards beneath my feet, wandering over the worn wood that covers the length of my childhood home. The mere sight of the familiar floor floods me with memories, and I fight to blink away the fleeting images of small feet atop big booted ones as they stepped in time to a familiar melody. I shake my

head, trying to rid myself the memory from it despite desperately wishing I could dwell in the past, seeing that my present isn't the most pleasant at the moment.

. . . sixteen, seventeen, eighteen—

I smile, ignoring the pain that pinches my skin.

Found you.

My stride is unsteady and stiff, sore muscles straining with each step towards the seemingly normal floorboard. I drop to my knees, biting my tongue against the pain, and claw at the wood with crimson-stained fingers I struggle to ignore.

The floor appears to be just as stubborn as I am, refusing to budge. I would have admired its resilience if it weren't a damn piece of *wood*.

I don't have time for this. I need to get out of here.

A frustrated sound tears from my throat before I blink at the board, blurting, 'I could have sworn you were the secret compartment. Are you not the nineteenth floorboard from the door?'

I'm staring daggers at the wood before a hysterical laugh slips past my lips, and I tip my head back to shake it at the ceiling. 'Plagues, now I'm talking to the *floor*,' I mutter, further proof that I'm losing my mind.

Although, it's not as if I have anyone else to talk to.

It's been four days since I stumbled back to my childhood home, haunted and half dead. And yet, both my mind and body are far from healed.

I may have dodged death with each swipe of the king's sword, but he still managed to kill a part of me that day after the final Trial. His words cut deeper than his blade ever could, slicing me with slivers of truths as he toyed with me, taunted me, told me of my father's death with a smile tugging at his lips.

'Wouldn't you like to know who it was that killed your father?'

A shiver snakes down my spine while the king's cold voice echoes through my skull.

'Let's just say that your first encounter with a prince wasn't when you saved Kai in the alley.''

If betrayal was a weapon, he bestowed it upon me that day, driving the blunt blade through my broken heart. I blow out a shaky breath, pushing away thoughts of the boy with gray eyes as piercing as the sword I watched him drive through my father's chest so many years ago.

Staggering to my feet, I shift my weight over the surrounding floorboards, listening for an indicating creak while mindlessly spinning the silver ring on my thumb. My body aches all over, my very bones feeling far too fragile. The wounds I earned from both the final Trial and my fight with the king were hastily tended to, the result of shaky fingers and silent sobs that left my vision blurry and stitches sloppy.

After limping from the Bowl Arena towards Loot Alley, I stumbled into the white shack I called home and the Resistance called headquarters. But I was greeted with emptiness. There were no familiar faces filling the secret room beneath my feet, leaving me with nothing but my pain and confusion.

I was alone – have been alone – left to clean up the mess that is my body, my brain, my bleeding heart.

The wood beneath me groans. I grin.

Once again I'm on the floor, prying up a beam to reveal a shadowy compartment beneath. I shake my head at myself, mumbling, 'It's the nineteenth floorboard from the *window*, not the door, Pae . . .'

I reach into the darkness, fingers curling round the unfamiliar hilt of a dagger. My heart aches more than my body, wishing to feel the swirling steel handle of my father's weapon against my palm.

But I chose the shedding of blood over sentiment when I threw my beloved blade into the king's throat.

And my only regret is that *he* found it, promising to return it only when he'd stabbed it into my back.

Empty blue eyes blink at me in the reflection of the shiny blade I lift it into the light, startling me enough to halt my hateful thoughts. My skin is splattered with slices, covered in cuts. I swallow at the sight of the gash traveling down the side of my neck, skim fingers over the jagged skin. Shaking my head, I slip the dagger into my boot, stowing away my scared reflection with it.

I spot a bow and its quiver of sharp arrows concealed in the compartment, and the shadow of a sad smile crosses my face at the memory of Father teaching me how to shoot, the gnarled tree behind our house my only target.

Slinging the bow and quiver across my back, I sift through the other weapons hidden beneath the floor. After tossing a few sharp throwing knives into my pack, joining the rations, water canteens, and crumpled shirt I'd hastily tucked inside, I struggle to my feet.

I've never felt so delicate, so damaged. The thought has me swelling with anger, has me snatching a knife from my waist and itching to plunge it into the worn, wooden wall before me. Searing pain shoots down my raised arm when the brand above my heart pulls taught with the movement.

A reminder. A representation of what I am. Or rather, what I'm not.

O for Ordinary.

I send the knife flying, plunging it into the wood with gritted teeth. The scar stings, gloating of its endless existence on my body.

'. . . *I will leave my mark on your heart, lest you forget who's broken it.'*

I stalk over to the blade, ready to yank it from the wall when the board beneath my foot creaks, drawing my attention. Despite knowing that flimsy floorboards are anything but foreign to houses in the slums, my curiosity has me bending to investigate.

If every creaky board were a compartment, our floor would be littered with them . . .

'I lift the wood, and my eyebrows do the same, shooting up my forehead in shock. I huff out a humorless laugh as I reach into the shadows of the compartment I didn't know existed.

Silly of me to think that the Resistance was the only secret Father kept from me.

My fingers brush worn leather before I pull out a large book, stuffed with papers that threaten to spill out.

I flip through it, recognizing the messy handwriting of a physician.

Father's journal.

I shove it into my pack, knowing I don't have the time or safety needed to study his work now. I've been here too long, spent too many days wounded and weak and worrying that I'll be found.

The Sight that witnessed me murder the king has likely displayed that image all over the kingdom. I need to get out of Ilya, and I've already wasted the head start *he* so graciously gave me.

I make my way to the door, ready to slip out and onto the streets where I can disappear into the chaos that is Loot. From there, I'll attempt to head across the Scorches to the city of Dor, where Elites don't exist and Ordinary is all they know.

Reaching for the door and the quiet street beyond—

I halt, hand outstretched.

Quiet.

It's nearly midday, meaning Loot and its surrounding streets should be a swarm of swearing merchants and squealing children as the slums buzz with color and commotion.

Something's not right . . .

The door shudders, something – someone – ramming into it from the outside. I jump back, eyes darting around the room. I contemplate ducking down the secret stairwell to the room beneath that held the Resistance meetings, but the thought of being cornered down there makes me queasy. That's when my gaze snaps to the fireplace, sighing in annoyance despite my current situation.

How do I always find myself in a chimney?

The door breaks open with a bang before I've barely shimmied halfway up the grimy wall, my feet planted In front of me while bricks dig into my back.

Brawny.

Only an Elite with extraordinary strength would be able to smash through my barricaded and bolted door so quickly. The sound of heavy boots has me figuring that five Imperials have just filed into my home.

'Don't just stand there. Search the place and convince me that you're useful.'

A shiver runs down my spine at the sound of that cool voice, the one I've heard sound like both a caress and a command. I stiffen, slipping slightly down the sooty wall.

He's here.

The voice that follows is gravely, belonging to an Imperial. 'You heard the Enforcer. Get a move on.'

The Enforcer.

I bite my tongue, whether to keep myself from letting out a bitter laugh or a scream, I'm not sure. My blood boils at the title, reminding me of everything he's done, every bit of evil he's committed in the shadow of the king. First for his father, and now for his brother – thanks to me ridding him of the former.

Except he's not thanking me. No, he's come to kill me instead.

'Maybe when I rid myself of you, I'll find my courage. So I'm giving you a head start.'

A lot of good his head start has done me.

I can't risk being heard scrambling up the chimney, so I wait, listening to heavy footsteps stomping through the house in search of me. My legs are beginning to shake, straining to hold me up while my every wound has me wincing in pain.

'Check the bookcases in the study. There should be a secret passage behind one,' the Enforcer commands dryly, sounding bored.

Once again, I find myself stiffening. A Resistance member must have confessed that little secret after he tortured it out of them. My pulse quickens at the thought of the fight after the final Trial in the Bowl when Ordinaries, Fatals, and Imperials clashed in a bloody battle.

A bloody battle that I still don't know the outcome of.

The steps of the Imperials grow distant, the sounds of their search softening as they head down the stairs and into the room beneath.

Quiet.

And yet, I know he's still in this room. Only a feeble amount of feet separate us. I can practically feel his presence, just as I've felt the heat of his body against mine, the heat of his gray gaze as it swept over me.

A floorboard creaks. He's close. I'm shaking with anger, revenge coursing through my blood and desperately wishing to spill his. It's a good thing I can't see his face because if I were to catch sight of one of his stupid dimples right now, I wouldn't be able to stop myself from trying to claw it from his face.

But I steady my breathing instead, knowing that if I fight him now, my fury won't be enough to beat him. And I intend to win when I finally face the Enforcer.

'I imagine you pictured my face when you threw

that knife.' His voice is quiet, considering, sounding far more like the boy I knew. Memories of him flood my mind, managing to make my heart race. 'Isn't that right, Paedyn?' And there it is. The edge is back in the Enforcer's voice, erasing Kai and leaving a commander.

My heart hammers against my rib cage.

He can't know I'm here. How could he possibly——?

The sound of a blade ripping from splintered wood tells me he yanked my knife out of the wall. I hear a familiar flicking noise and can practically picture him mindlessly flipping the weapon in his hand.

'Tell me, darling, do you think of me often?' His voice is a murmur as if his lips were pressed against my ear. I shiver, knowing exactly what that feels like.

If he knows I'm here then why hasn't he——?

'Do I haunt your dreams, plague your thoughts, like you do mine?'

My breath hitches.

So he doesn't know I'm here, not for certain.

His admission told me as much.

As an Ordinary who was trained and tailored into a Psychic, my father taught me to read people, to gather information and observations in a matter of seconds.

And I've had far more than a matter of seconds to

read Kai Azer.

I've seen through his many masks and facades, glimpsing the boy beneath and growing to know him, care for him. And with all the betrayal now between us, I know he wouldn't declare dreaming of me if he knew I was drinking in every word.

I hear the humor in his voice as he sighs. 'Where are you, Little Psychic?'

His nickname is laughable, seeing that he and the rest of the kingdom now know I'm anything but. Anything but Elite.

Nothing but Ordinary.

Soot stings my nose and I have to clamp my hand over it to hold in a sneeze, reminding me of my many nights thieving from the stores lining Loot before escaping through cramped chimneys.

Cramped. Trapped. Suffocating.

My eyes dart across the bricks surrounding me in the darkness. The space is so small, so stuffy, so very easily making me panic.

Calm down.

Claustrophobia chooses the worst times to claw to the surface and remind me of my helplessness.

Breathe.

I do. Deeply. The hand still clamped over my nose smells faintly of metal – sharp and strong and stinging my nose.

Blood.

I pull the shaky hand away from my face, and though I can't see the crimson staining my fingers, I can practically feel it clinging to me. There's still blood crusted under my cracked nails, and I don't know whether it's mine, the king's, or . . .

I suck in a breath, trying to pull myself together. The Enforcer looms far too close to me, pacing the floor, wood groaning beneath him with each step.

Getting caught because I started sobbing would be equally as embarrassing as getting caught for sneezing.

And I refuse to do either.

At some point, the Imperials stomp back into the room beneath me. 'No sign of her, Your Highness.'

There's a long pause before his highness sighs. 'Just as I thought. You're all useless.' His next words are sharper than the blade he flips casually in his hand. 'Get out.'

The Imperials don't waste a single second before scrambling towards the door and away from him. I don't blame them.

But he's still here, leaving nothing but silence to

stretch between us. I have a hand clamped over my nose again, and the smell of blood combined with the cramped chimney has my head spinning.

Memories flood my mind – my body caked in blood, my screams as I tried to scrub it away, only managing to stain my skin a sickening red. The sight and smell of so much blood made me sick, made me think of my father bleeding out in my arms, of Adena doing the same.

Adena.

Tears prick my eyes again, forcing me to blink away the image of her lifeless body in the sandy Pit. The metallic stench of blood fills my nose, and I can't stand to smell it, to look at it, to feel it—

Breathe.

A heavy sigh cuts through my thoughts. He sounds as tired as I feel. 'It's a good thing you're not here,' he says softly, a tone I never thought I'd hear from him again. 'Because I still haven't found my courage.'

And then my home bursts into flames.

CHAPTER 2

Rai

Flames lick at my heels as I leisurely make my way to the door.

Waves of heat crash into my back; wisps of smoke cling to my clothing. I step outside into the cloudy afternoon, now further polluted by the billowing clouds of smoke wafting into the sky.

My lips twitch at the look of shock on my Imperials' faces, accompanied by the unhinged jaws they fight to clamp shut as flames consume the house behind me. Their gazes slowly flick to me, managing to reach as high as my collar before they're shifting uncomfortably on their feet.

They still when I stride towards them with ease.

They think I've gone mad.

Glass shatters when a window bursts behind me, sending shards of sharp edges scattering the street. The Imperials' flinch, covering their faces. The sight makes me smile.

Maybe they're right. Maybe I have gone mad.

Mad with worry, with rage, with betrayal.

The tension continuously coiling through my body seems to be the only constant in my life, resulting in stiffened shoulders and a clenched jaw. My fingers drum against the dagger at my side, tempting me to take out my frustration on one of the many useless Imperials.

I trace the swirling steel on the hilt, the pattern familiar beneath my fingertips. How could I forget the dagger that's been held against my throat so many times?

How could I forget the dagger that I pulled from my father's severed neck?

It's been five days since I saw the hilt of this very weapon protruding from the king's throat. Five days to grieve, and yet, I haven't shed a single tear. Five days to prepare, and yet, no plan will truly free me from her. Five days to simply be Kitt and Kai – brothers before we became king and Enforcer.

And now her head start is up.

Though it seems that she used it wisely – took advantage of my weakness, my cowardice, my *feelings* for her – and ran. I spin to face the flames, watching the colorful chaos as fire consumes her home in red, orange, thick black smoke and—

Silver.

I blink, squinting through suffocating smoke at the collapsing roof. But there's nothing there, no hint of the shimmer I saw a moment ago. I run a hand through my hair before pressing the heels of my palms against tired eyes.

Yes, I've truly gone mad.

'Sir!'

I drop my hands, slowly fixing my gaze on the Imperial brave enough to shout at me. He clears his throat, likely regretting that decision. 'I, uh, I think I saw something, Your Highness.'

He points to the flaming roof, smoke shifting as a figure stumbles through the flames. A figure with silver hair.

So she is here.

I can't seem to decide whether I'm relieved or not.

'Bring her to me.'

My command rings out, and the Imperials don't miss a beat. And, apparently, neither does she. I barely catch a glimpse of her before she jumps off the edge of the crumbling roof and onto the neighboring one, legs bounding as soon as she finds her footing.

Imperials run down the street below, Brawnies and Shields rendered utterly useless as she jumps from roof to roof. I comb a hand through my hair before dragging it down my face, unsurprised by their incompetence.

I flip the knife I'd yanked from the wall in my hand before taking off down the street, quickly catching up with my Imperials. I feel each of their powers buzzing under my skin, begging to be released. But their abilities are useless to me unless I can get her on the ground, making me regret not bringing a Tele that could set her on the street before me with nothing but a thought.

She can only stay on the rooftops if she's able to jump between them. And that's why, with the flick of my wrist, I send the knife flying towards her.

I watch as it meets its mark, slicing through her thigh as she leaps. Her cry of pain makes me flinch, an action that is as frustrating as it is foreign to me.

She hits the flat roof hard, rolling in a feeble attempt to lessen the fall. I watch as she staggers to her feet, blood streaming down her leg. Her features are fuzzy from this distance, and I can almost pretend that she is simply a forgetful figure limping to the edge of a roof.

She's no fool. She knows she can't make the jump.

My gaze snaps to the Imperials' gawking up at her. 'Must I do everything for you?' My voice is cold. 'Go get her.'

But then my eyes wander back up to the roof. Empty.

Foolish of me to think she'd make this easy.

'Find her,' I bark, gritting my teeth against a slew of curses. The Imperials split up, sprinting in opposite directions down the streets I ensured would be practically empty for this exact reason. A thief's ability to blend in is alarming, allowing them to get swallowed in chaos, lost in a crowd. And she would do just that if I hadn't cleared Loot for the day.

I stride down the street, glancing into the adjacent alleys jutting off it. Muffled shouts ring out, echoing off the rundown homes and shops. I silently continue my search, feet faltering when I spot a figure slumped at the end of a shadowed alley.

My body tenses. I turn toward the silhouette, each step warier than the last. But it's not long before recognition has my pace quickening. I crouch beside the

Imperial, eyes wandering over his once white uniform, now soaked with blood. Scarlet seeps from a throwing knife buried deep in his chest, oozing over the crisp folds of his uniform.

She is a vicious little thing.

My fingers are at his throat, checking for a pulse despite knowing I won't feel its familiar beat. I sigh, dropping my head into my hands. My whole body feels heavy with exhaustion, weighed down by my worries.

I buried someone who tried to kill her once.

Simply because I knew it was something she would have wanted. I carried Sadie's dead body through the dark Whispers Forest during that first Trial because I knew Paedyn was falling apart when I left her to spin that ring on her thumb. If it were up to me, I would have never buried the body of someone who tried to kill her. But I wasn't thinking of myself when I'd done it.

Death is familiar to me, both friend and foe, and far too frequent in my life. But for her, death is devastation, no matter its victim.

I imagine she's spinning that ring on her thumb at this very moment, biting the inside of her cheek as she forces herself to run from the man she just killed rather than dig him a grave like I know she desperately wishes to.

'She would have buried you if she weren't so busy running from me, you know,' I murmur to the body beside me, confirming that I have, in fact, gone mad. I lift the Imperial's white mask from his face, giving me a better view of his glassy brown eyes before I brush his lids closed. 'So the least I can do is bury you for her.'

I'd never given a second thought to what became of my soldier's bodies. And yet, here I am, hauling a man over my shoulder because of a girl who despises doling out death. I grunt under the Imperial's weight, wondering why the hell I'm even bothering with this.

What has she done to me?

His limp body swings over my shoulder with every step I take.

Will her grave be the next I dig?

Acknowledgements

It would be a lie to say I haven't skimmed through several of my favorite author's acknowledgments, trying to work out the best way to go about this. Because I'm convinced there is a secret formula to follow, one that keeps you – the lovely reader – engaged while I – the rambling author – attempt to express my admiration for the people who made this book possible. And maybe by the end of this, you can let me know if I figured it out or not?

To say I left a piece of my heart between the folds of these pages would be far too soppy for my liking. But *Powerful* means so much to me. Writing this story following the release of *Powerless* felt more than daunting. I so desperately wanted this story to be Adena's alone, and the weight of not doing her justice was crushing. But within the span of a mere month, this novella truly wrote itself. Though, something far greater was also achieved when I typed that final word into the manuscript. I proved something to myself:

My story—my dream—did not end when I finished *Powerless* at the age of 18. And I've now gained the courage to keep dreaming. Keep writing. Keep doing what I love.

Alright, enough about me. I can confidently say that I wouldn't get the chance to write acknowledgements if it weren't for a handful of incredible people. To start, I have the great privilege of working hand-in-hand with not one, but two incredible Simon & Schuster teams. Even with my scarily over-active imagination, I could have never dreamed of having a group of people in both the US and UK that care so deeply about me and my stories. I wish I could give each of you a kiss on the cheek but given that several thousand miles separate most of us, I will have to settle for typing your name with the upmost admiration.

Starting with the lovely UK team, it seems only right to begin with Yasmin Morrissey. As one of my brave editors, you have endured countless voice memos, emails, and zoom calls about all things *Powerless*. You have been there through every stage of this book, and I cannot thank you enough for your constant support.

Even my imposter syndrome and self-criticism are no match for you! I genuinely fear what would become of me without your diligence, and I look forward to many more lengthy voice memos in the future!

But there are several other members of the UK team I have the honor to thank, starting with Rachel Denwood and Ali Dougal — my managing and publishing directors. Laura Hough and Danielle Wilson have championed my work with UK retailers while Loren Catana, my in-house Designer, came up with the gorgeous cover design for *Powerful*. Miya Elkerton and Olivia Horrox in Marketing, along with Jess Dean and Ellen Abernethy in Publicity. The fantastic rights team, led by Maud Sepult and Emma Martinez who have found incredible international homes for *Powerless*. Last – but certainly not least – Nicholas Hayne and everyone else. Thank you.

As for my equally lovely US team, I must shower Nicole Ellul with immense thanks and admiration. Being my other fearless editor is no simple task. You have helped guide me so graciously through each publication process, and your faith in my work is appreciated more than you know. Thank you for every idea and ounce of input that has made this series what it now is. Your

enthusiasm alone is an inspiration to me.

And to the rest of the marvelous US crew, I have Jenica Nasworthy to thank for keeping everything organized as my managing editor. But there are several others who deserve a huge, general thank-you as well. Chava Wolin, Lucy Cummins, Hilary Zarycky, Alyza Liu, Justin Chanda, Kendra Levine, Nicole Russo, Emily Ritter, and Brandon MacDonald – you all are incredible at what you do. Thank you.

At this time, feel free to take a break from my ramblings to drool over the gorgeous artwork and map in the front of this book. And, yes, the rumors are true. It is all hand-drawn by the insanely talented Jordan Elliot. I cannot think of a better person to bring my world to life, and I am incredibly honored to continue working together. Here's to more jaw-dropping art!

To my unflinching attorney/agent, Lloyd Jassin. Thank you for helping navigate me through this world of publishing – I cannot imagine tackling any of this without you. You are a pleasure to work with, and I hope to continue doing so for many years to come.

Besides the incredible S&S teams who helped assemble *Powerful*, there are several others at work behind the scenes. And I happen to be related to those individuals. Firstly, I can humbly admit that none of these dreams would have come true if it weren't for my parents. Mom and Dad, you have supported me every step of the way, believed in me when I found it hard to believe in myself. Thank you for trusting your little girl enough to let her pursue this passion. I am so blessed to have you both, but especially a mother who happily juggles being my confidant, assistant, and bookkeeper.

Being the runt of the family, there are a few older siblings to acknowledge. Jessie, Nikki, Josh – you have all supported me in your own ways. I deeply appreciate every encouraging text and proverbial pat on the back. Thank you, Foos.

Aside from my family, there are several friends who ensured I stayed sane during this writing process. I would like to give a general thank-you to Ivy and Ella – you are the reason I survived both high school and this current, crazy stage of life. I love you endlessly. As for my beloved Olivia, Powerful would not be out in the world if it weren't for you. Scheming up this story at a dirty coffeeshop table is one of my fondest memories, and I hope to continue conspiring with you. Thank you for putting up with my alarmingly lengthy messages. You are truly the voice of the people, Pookie!

Now onto the daunting task of attempting to express my feelings for a certain boy. Zac, to say you are my rock would be an understatement. Thank you for every bit of encouragement and willingness to help. Whether it's cooking me a meal or offering a shoulder to cry on, I can always rely on your comfort. You are truly my fictional boy incarnate, and I hope to write our story one day.

As stated in the back of *Powerless*, I'd like to thank the One who gifted me my love of words and the desire to write. I truly would not be where I am today without my Lord and Savior, and I thank God for the opportunity He has given me.

Now it is your turn, dear reader. Did I hold your attention up until this point? Were you waiting for me to finally acknowledge you? Because it is all thanks to you that I made it to this very page. I am honored to be on this journey together, and even more so that you took the time to read my story. You are my inspiration, my reason for every word. And I hope to hold your attention for many years to come.

Here's to more dreams, and the stories they create.

XO, Lauren

Hunted. Hunter.
Destined for each other.

Powerless

INTERNATIONAL BESTSELLING AUTHOR
LAUREN ROBERTS

**The first in the instant
New York Times bestselling series**

Traitor. Tormented.
Destined for each other.

Reckless

INTERNATIONAL BESTSELLING AUTHOR OF *POWERLESS*

LAUREN ROBERTS

**Be swept away by the second
heart-racing instalment in this bestselling
and sizzling fantasy romance trilogy**